Contents

Yui

Komachi

Yukino

My Youth Romantic Comedy Is Wrong, As I Expected

Iroha Isshiki

Happy Birthday,
Iroha-chan!

MY YOUTH R♥MANTIC C☺MEDY iS WRØNG, AS I EXPECTED

Wataru Watari
Illustration **Ponkan⑧**

VOLUME
14.5

YEN ON
NEW YORK

MY YOUTH ROMANTIC COMEDY IS WRONG, AS I EXPECTED Vol. 14.5
WATARU WATARI
Illustration by Ponkan⑧

Translation by Jennifer Ward
Cover art by Ponkan⑧

YAHARI ORE NO SEISHUN LOVE COME WA MACHIGATTEIRU.
Vol. 14.5 by Wataru WATARI
© 2011 Wataru WATARI
Illustration by PONKAN⑧
All rights reserved.
Original Japanese edition published by SHOGAKUKAN.
English translation rights in the United States of America, Canada, the United Kingdom, Ireland, Australian and New Zealand arranged with SHOGAKUKAN through Tuttle-Mori Agency, Inc.

English translation © 2022 by Yen Press, LLC

Yen On
150 West 30th Street, 19th Floor
New York, NY 10001

Visit us at yenpress.com
facebook.com/yenpress
twitter.com/yenpress
yenpress.tumblr.com
instagram.com/yenpress

First Yen On Edition: October 2022
Edited by Yen On Editorial: Anna Powers
Designed by Yen Press Design: Wendy Chan

Yen On is an imprint of Yen Press, LLC.
The Yen On name and logo are trademarks of Yen Press, LLC.

Library of Congress Cataloging-in-Publication Data
Names: Watari, Wataru, author. | Ponkan 8, illustrator.
Title: My youth romantic comedy is wrong, as I expected / Wataru Watari ; illustration by Ponkan 8.
Other titles: Yahari ore no seishun love come wa machigatteiru. English
Description: New York : Yen On, 2016–
Identifiers: LCCN 2016005816 | ISBN 9780316312295 (v. 1 : pbk.) | ISBN 9780316396011 (v. 2 : pbk.) |
    ISBN 9780316318068 (v. 3 : pbk.) | ISBN 9780316318075 (v. 4 : pbk.) | ISBN 9780316318082 (v. 5 : pbk.) |
    ISBN 9780316411868 (v. 6 : pbk.) | ISBN 9781975384166 (v. 6.5 : pbk.) | ISBN 9781975384128 (v. 7 : pbk.) |
    ISBN 9781975384159 (v. 7.5 : pbk.) | ISBN 9781975384135 (v. 8 : pbk.) | ISBN 9781975384142 (v. 9 : pbk.) |
    ISBN 9781975384111 (v. 10 : pbk.) | ISBN 9781975384173 (v. 10.5 : pbk.) | ISBN 9781975324988 (v. 11 : pbk.) |
    ISBN 9781975324995 (v. 12 : pbk.) | ISBN 9781975325008 (v. 13 : pbk.) | ISBN 9781975325015 (v. 14 : pbk.) |
    ISBN 9781975347932 (v. 14.5 : pbk.)
Subjects: | CYAC: Optimism—Fiction. | School—Fiction.
Classification: LCC PZ7.1.W396 My 2016 | DDC [Fic]—dc23
LC record available at http://lccn.loc.gov/2016005816

ISBNs: 978-1-9753-4793-2 (paperback)
       978-1-9753-4794-9 (ebook)

1 2022

LSC-C

Printed in the United States of America

MY YOUTH R♥MANTIC C☺MEDY iS WRØNG, AS I EXPECTED

fourteen and a half

Cast of Characters

Hachiman Hikigaya........... The main character. High school second-year. Twisted personality.

Yukino Yukinoshita........... Captain of the Service Club. Perfectionist.

Yui Yuigahama.................. Hachiman's classmate. Tends to worry about what other people think.

Saika Totsuka.................... In tennis club. Very cute. A boy, though.

Saki Kawasaki.................. Hachiman's classmate. Sort of a delinquent type.

Hayato Hayama.................. Hachiman's classmate. Popular. In the soccer club.

Yumiko Miura.................... Hachiman's classmate. Reigns over the girls in class as queen bee.

Hina Ebina........................ Hachiman's classmate. Part of Miura's clique, but a slash fangirl.

Iroha Isshiki..................... Manager of the soccer club. First-year student who was elected student council president.

Haruno Yukinoshita.......... Yukino's older sister. In university.

Komachi Hikigaya.............. Hachiman's little sister. In her third year in middle school.

Always and forevermore, **Komachi Hikigaya** wants a sister-in-law.

I think it was Sojun Ikkyuu who wrote the poem "Every New Year is a milestone in your journey to the underworld."

A wise saying. Truly a wise saying. The wise thing about it is how it's so, like, wise, man. The fact that his name literally means "taking a break" is another nugget of wisdom.

Nothing beats a holiday. That's such a wonderful appellation, Godiego would be raving about what a beautiful name it is.

Most events for which people say "Happy this!" or "Happy that!"— and I don't just mean New Year's, but also birthdays and graduations and whatnot—aren't actually that happy, since they involve the passage of time.

All the events celebrated in society are ultimately portents of the end. Getting one year older is a countdown to the end of your life, and it's fair to say the celebration of graduation indicates a sort of expulsion. These days, when an idol group gets fired, they'll even call it "graduation" to make it sound pretty. Once you start thinking that way, it's no longer an auspicious occasion at all. The only happy or lucky thing going on here is my happy-go-lucky brain. *Kya-ha!* Lucky me! Time to have another normal year!

And so, on that note, I'd been enthusiastically committed to making like Sojun Ikkyuu and lazing New Year's away. *Don't rush, don't rush, a break here, a break there…* But in spite of that, this *purimiamu Japaniizu burando* product automatically celebrates the *Niuu Iyaa* on its own, no mess, no fuss! Aw shucks, spewing gratuitous English like a shopping channel when I can't actually speak English is *sooo* Japanese…

In the end, Komachi dragged me along for the traditional New Year's visit to the shrine.

We met up with Yukinoshita and Yuigahama at Inage Sengen Shrine to do New Year's-y stuff like drawing fortunes, and then we ran into Miura and her friends, so Yuigahama joined them, and Komachi said she'd forgotten to buy a protection charm and went back…

Long story short, after being abandoned, Yukinoshita and I headed straight home.

Although it wasn't far at all and didn't take that long—it was just a few stops on the train—each and every moment lingers so vividly in my memory. I don't think I'll be able to easily forget the timid pressure hanging on my sleeve at odd moments, or her small hand, lifted up just slightly for a wave when we parted ways.

And so my New Year's finally came to a close.

After being swept along in the waves of shrinegoers (without being scolded from a distance), I ended the New Year's-appropriate events smoothly, and I returned to my empty home.

My parents must have gone out somewhere. I started nodding off while in the *kotatsu*, the family cat in my arms, as I waited for Komachi's return.

This is it… This is the right way to spend your New Year's…

There's no need at all to be bumping into girls first thing in the New Year and get your heart beating out of your chest. You've got to let Mr. Heart take a break in the New Year, too! Well, except that if he does, I'll die.

× × ×

A hard *tk* sound made me open my eyes. It seemed I'd actually fallen asleep while lazing in the *kotatsu*. When I jolted upright, Komachi was there, sitting at the corner diagonal from me, looking at me with displeasure. She pushed one of the mugs on the table over to me.

I accepted it with gratitude. "…Oh, thanks… Welcome home. You're early."

"That's what Komachi would like to say, though…" A dispirited half smile crossed her face, and then she took a slurp of her coffee and casually leaned her weight on the *kotatsu* to ask, "…So, Bro. How was it?"

"Nothing much. Normal," I answered carelessly, not sure what she was getting at.

Komachi waved a hand like, *No way, no way.* "Nah, nah. Normal? You're not a middle schooler in a rebellious phase."

"U-uh-huh… And neither are you, if you're pointing that out…" *If I may say so of my own sister, she tends to adopt strangely long-term views. Like, it's kinda housewife-ish.*

That's what I was thinking when Komachi inclined herself forward and said something an auntie would say. "You and Yukino walked back together, right? Nothing happened?"

"If just walking back together was enough to cause an incident, I'd be worried what the world is coming to. What do you think they make elementary schoolers walk in groups these days for? You need more danger awareness."

"Whoa, there it is. Don't give me that, okay?" She sighed like she found our conversation entirely taxing, turning to the New Year's TV show as if she was trying to remove me from her sight.

The annual New Year's show was basically the same every year, showing happy scenes appropriate for the occasion, like couples who had just signed their marriage papers or babies who were born on the New Year.

"I wanted to get things cleaned up last year…but at this rate, maybe it won't happen this year, either…" Komachi sighed.

"What? You mean spring cleaning?" I asked her.

"Yeah, I'm talking about my garbrother."

"You're not gonna be able to throw me out that easy. Everyone's all about going green and recycling lately," I quipped, though I admit it was not my best.

"How dare you...," Komachi muttered scarily, like a certain young environmentalist.

Oh dear, what frightful use of language... Has she gone delinquent? I trembled in fear as I eyed Komachi.

But it seemed she was off on her own worrying about something else. "Ahhh... My big bro really is a garbro. Even if Komachi somehow managed to get him married, he might wreck it immediately and have to move back home, which would double the work for me..."

Komachi's brother complex is reaching dangerous levels, if she's thinking about her brother's marriage before her own. Or maybe it's my dignity as an older brother that's reaching dangerous lows, for having my little sister worry about my marriage. I do feel like in this case, the smoothest course of action would be for us sketchy siblings to just get married instead—but legally speaking in this nation, that might be the most dangerous of all, so maybe we'll have to pass on that. Damn you, rule of law!

As I was burning with the urge to revolt, Komachi was getting fired up about something else. "In Komachi terms, though, it's not like there's no candidates for sister-in-law..."

"Hey, cut it out? Please don't come up with candidates for such personal stuff without the permission of the guy in question?"

"Komachi really does think the strongest sister candidate is...Yukino, I guess..."

She's not listening. If I engage with this nonsense, my New Year's will be wasted. I leaned toward the TV to end the conversation.

But then I got a poke-poke in my side. "Bro, are you listening? Komachi's trying to have a serious talk." My instincts as a big brother kicked in, and I automatically switched into listening mode. "If Yukino was my sister-in-law, you could become a househusband. Consider it in terms of your lifetime income."

"Don't just casually call my defeat on lifetime income before the game is over. You should imagine a brighter future for your brother."

"This is bright, though. It's so bright, Komachi can't see anything, like Solar Flare. Which is why I can say it's basically nothing."

Apparently, I've been borrowing Tien Shinhan's moves without even realizing it. So it's that hard to see, huh...?

While my shoulders were quietly slumping, Komachi was raising a fist high in the air. "And besides, Komachi figures Yukino would support Komachi, too. So Komachi will do household chores instead of you, too! Isn't that great, Bro?! Finally, the NEET lifestyle you always dreamed of!"

"I don't need that... You two should just get married... That seems like it could get you places, too, so Big Bro will stay right here at home...," I said.

Komachi broke into a kind smile, then said gently, "It's okay, Bro. Just as long as you're there for Komachi..."

Why's she suddenly overflowing with benevolence...? She's totally treating me like a pet. I hate it... Maybe starting tomorrow, I should start eating kitty food along with Kamakura to get myself used to it.

I was having a glaring match with Kamakura in preparation for the inevitable doomsday war over kitty treats when Komachi scooped the cat up in her arms. Stroking Kamakura as he purred on her lap, she decided to drop a bomb. "Well, if that's what we're going for, Haruno also has similar terms."

"Hey now, that one's scary. And you're scary, too, for being able to imagine her as a sister." I'm a dreamer myself, and even I make sure never to imagine things like that. Komachi is way too reckless with her life... Does she have ninety-nine green mushrooms or something?

Komachi slurped at her coffee as she continued to soar on the wings of imagination. "What if Saki was my big sister? That's another option."

"No. And this one is totally unrelated to your last suggestion."

"But her little sister has to come, too. Komachi's heard she's very cute." With a smug chuckle, she laid down the most powerful card of the Kawasaki family deck and ended her turn. I didn't know if Komachi had ever actually met Keika, but between Kawa-something and Taishi, at least one of them would probably want to tell people about her. Keika is just that charming and cute.

"...............I'll think abo— Whoa, there! Hey, then Taishi would come, too. Forget it, forget it. Not happening." When you get to be an ultimate duelist of my level, you're sensitive to trap cards. I just barely managed to evade it. I'm not saying anything about Kawa-something as an individual—but as an older brother, I can't let Taishi get close to Komachi.

But Komachi must have picked up on the effect Keika had on me, as she folded her arms with a *hmm* and drew her next card. "I see... You do have decent compatibility with younger girls, huh...? Oh, then how about, like, Rumi-chan?"

"Rumi-Rumi's, like... She's my idol. I don't see her as anything more. It's more like I want to do idol stuff with her and share in the passion... She makes me want to support her in a pure way."

"Hmm, it's a little creepy how seriously you're taking this... And the way you put it sounds so intense, it actually freaks me out..." I'd meant to explain myself with the most wholehearted, utmost sincerity, but now Komachi was leaning away from me.

She seemed to resign herself eventually, letting out a deep sigh. "So younger is no good, too... Then going the other way...how about Miss Hiratsuka?"

The moment she said that, the air between us turned to ice.

The playful exchange we'd been having took a one-eighty as I was compelled to envision this somewhat realistic responsibility. You couldn't joke about this stuff casually; it was too heavy for that.

Komachi must have felt that keenly, too. She let her head fall sadly. "Sorry. Maybe Komachi went a little too far with that one."

"Yeah. Let's pretend that didn't happen. I'm sure Miss Hiratsuka will find her happiness. Not like I know." With a distant look in my eyes, I prayed. *Hurry...! Hurry, someone take her! Don't wait! One wrong move, and I just might snap her up!*

For a while, the sound of the TV attempted to fill the hollow silence in the wordless living room. We slurped at our coffees, then sighed simultaneously.

After spending some time with our eyes on the TV, Komachi suddenly spoke again. "Well, so long as you're happy, Komachi's fine with it. Oh, and that was worth a lot of Komachi points." She smiled, and I dipped my head ever so slightly in a voiceless response.

Nevertheless, **Komachi Hikigaya** won't give up on getting a sister-in-law.

The season was still midwinter. The new calendar had only finally ticked out one day's worth of time.

The day after going to visit the shrine, I accomplished the promise I'd made Yuigahama there—to go buy a birthday present for Yukinoshita—and then hurried home on my own.

My breath looked even whiter than usual, maybe because it was just that heavy and deep. My exhalation under the cold sky came slowly, unlike my restlessly moving feet. It was just one breath, but it formed a trail you could mistake for smoke, wafting along just a moment before it disappeared in the wind. The inclining rays of the sunset gave it a ruddy color, with an added flicker of neon blue, before it eventually melted into the darkness. It was like all the sighs of the day condensed into one.

The time spent shopping and having a trivial conversation with Yuigahama, for example, and those little moments that brought us closer—they were a lot like the color of the sunset. But then running into Haruno and Hayama had felt weirdly tense, like the indigo blue of the darkening sky. Then after that, when Yukinoshita and her mother had come, I'd sensed the black of night.

I looked up at the sky, as if searching for a ray of light far in the distance, where the curtain had descended.

I couldn't know what I would eventually see there, but even so, my feet never stopped, making at least a little progress toward where I should go, to the place I should return, to the answers I should come to.

That's how I—how we have walked through this past year and begun the new one.

Thinking about that now, it hadn't been much time since the beginning of the new year, but things had gone pretty well for me.

I'd managed to finish shopping with Yuigahama and hand over Yukinoshita's present without any problems, after all. You could call that mission complete. You could get a reward to use on a gacha pull.

I had mission-completed so perfectly, I wouldn't be surprised to hear the voice of a younger girl cheering, *You did it!* Love those girls...

The younger girl in my life is the type to have no problem saying something like *Wanna spend it now? Act now, and if you pull enough times, you're guaranteed a five-star!*...

X   X   X

After our family had finished our New Year's traditions, it was just Komachi, Kamakura, and me in the living room.

Drinking the after-dinner coffee that Komachi had made for me at the *kotatsu*, I was just about to attend to some lucky bag gacha when Komachi, who was petting Kamakura, cleared her throat with an *ahem*.

"...Well then, Bro, how'd it go?"

I understood what she was trying to ask. She'd come with us for half the shopping trip that day. She'd absconded afterwards, probably in some needless attempt to be considerate...

In other words, she was asking how things had gone after she'd left. This was the same as that time I'd come back from the shrine.

So then it was self-evident that my answer would also be the same thing. "Nothing much. Normal," I said.

Komachi breathed a big sigh. "Aghhhhh. Listen, Bro. In Komachi terms, Yui is in one of the top spots on the list of big sister candidates, you know? There aren't that many people who are so perfect for being a big sister as her these days, okay?"

"Uh, like I said before, cut it out. No more of this 'sister-in-law candidates' list that completely ignores what I actually want. Send it for immediate disposal. Learn from the prime minister's cherry-blossom-event invitation list." By introducing such social satire, I'm emphasizing that I have an active interest in politics and that I'm aiming to be Chiba prefectural governor next term (hi, that's me). We will build an even greater Chiba...

But it seemed Komachi still wasn't really interested in politics, as she didn't listen to my election manifesto for prefectural governor and moved the discussion along without me. "Komachi thinks if Yui were my sister-in-law, she'd also be a very, very good bride for you, Bro."

"No, no, no," I said, immediately raising my hand. *Objection!* "Obviously, Yuigahama would be a good bride no matter who she was married to. There's no need to limit her partner to me in this. Therefore, proposals under the presently established conditions are not worthy of debate. Aaand I take the W."

The disgust on Komachi's face seemed pretty real. "Whoa, you're so obnoxious... This is the reason Komachi's struggling to set you up, you know?"

When I heard her tone turn a little serious, my head drooped. "Yeah..." I had no choice but to settle down.

Satisfied to see my contrition, Komachi collected herself and continued. "Ummm, so then, the second-choice competitor..."

"Huhhh... Your drafting session is still going?" I said, more than half weirded out.

But Komachi was actually puffing up with pride. "Of course! Komachi still has lots more cards to play, you know!"

"Hey? Could you stop talking about my marriage like this is a duel? Even if you send your big bro to the graveyard, you can't summon a big sister. The summon cost of a wife is high, and immediate divorce is possible, too." On my end, I laid the three cards of *divorce, division of property*, and *alimony* on the table and ended my turn. And now, if she activated the trap card *mismatch of personalities*, the *divorce and return to parents' house* combo was complete.

But Komachi ignored that combo, used her hands to set an invisible box to the side, and continued. "Hmm, well, leaving that aside... why don't we go off the beaten path here and say Miura?"

"That's *way* off the beaten path... No way, never gonna happen. Impossible. This is Miura, okay? Never gonna happen. Take this a little more seriously, Komachi, even if you're joking. Maybe this is just idle chitchat to you, but your brother's future is hanging on this."

"Wow, you really shot that one down, Bro... It makes it sound like you actually really like her..."

Well, I do like that idea quite a bit, for what it is... She is a good person... But if I said that, even as a joke, Komachi would jump on it, so I cleared my throat with a *gefum, gefum.* "Well, whatever I think about her, she really hates me, so..."

"Yeah, I think most people hate you, so leaving that aside...," she said casually, once again placing an invisible box at the edge of the table.

I wasn't about to let that one go. "Hey now? I mean, I know that, so I'll let that one go." If she kept putting things aside like that, she'd wind up with a huge pile of invisible boxes.

"I feel like Miura would be a good mom, though," said Komachi.

"Yeah, she would. And her kids would get really long mullets. And then around fifth grade, she'd go and dye their hair and cause a dispute with their school."

"Yeahhh...the type you see at the discount store a lot before they get married, and then once they have families, they're at the department store..."

"Uh, that's Kawasaki, if anything. Miura's more fashionable than that. She'd normally go to the outlet mall and then once a year go to Isetan or something."

"I don't get the difference... Then on to the next candidate," Komachi said with a sigh, sweeping that discussion aside. She slurped at her coffee for a moment before saying, as if it had just occurred to her, "Oh, then what about Ebina?"

That wasn't a name I was expecting. I fell into thought. "Ahhh... Well, we're both totally disinterested. But since we're not involved with each other at all and don't interfere with each other's lives, maybe it wouldn't be out of the question. With the assumption that we wouldn't have a domestic life together, if we shared the benefits in terms of societal lifestyle, I feel like it would be contractually viable," I said.

Komachi made a sour-looking *eugh* face. "The way you say that is way too *modern couple*... By the way, what kind of benefits do you mean?"

"It's apparently easier to get a loan if you're married. Then there's the tax consolidation, exemplified by the dependent tax exemption. Additionally, you can use it as a shield against the harsh social criticism singles receive," I said, presenting my smattering of knowledge on the matter.

Komachi seemed taken aback, her expression gradually turning sadder before becoming pity. "............You don't think your view of marriage is totally broken, Bro?"

"I mean, this is ultimately just one example. I'm merely saying this is one progressive way of thinking about it, you know?" I may not look it, but I'm aiming for future prefectural governor of Chiba. I have to show acceptance toward more liberal lifestyles, not only the traditional image of a couple.

After hearing some more of the Chiba Prefectural Governor Election Manifesto I hadn't mentioned before, Komachi started pondering. Then she seemed almost convinced. "I see... Well, worst case, if you wind up marrying Hayama, Komachi will be understanding."

"No, not happening. Not Hayama. More important than sex or whatever, our personalities wouldn't work together," I answered in seconds, remembering to be inclusive in the process. So that I wouldn't get whacked by the Treasured Tool that was the Staff of Political Correctness, I rejected it for the reason that, ultimately, Hayama and I were not compatible.

Komachi must have understood that as well, because she moved on to the next candidate. "Oh, then what about To—?"

"I love him," I answered in seconds. This was beyond logic. Forget Chiba prefectural governor—I was ready to shoot straight to national politics and revise the law.

But I must have been a bit too enthusiastic. "That was too fast, Bro," said Komachi, aghast. "I still haven't said the whole name... I was about to say Tobe..."

"Oh, really...? Wait, who's Tobe?" I said.

Komachi sighed deeply once more. The room was too warm for that slow exhalation to turn into white mist, but I could still see in it the many colors to express her feelings. "Well, so long as you're happy, Bro, Komachi's fine with anything."

"Then I've got to make you happy first, since that's my ticket to happiness. That was worth a lot of points, in Hachiman terms."

After I stole her bit, Komachi gave me a puzzled look. But just for an instant, before she broke into an exasperated smile. "There's still a long road ahead...," she said with deep resignation, then took the mugs, stood from the *kotatsu* with a *hup*, and headed to the kitchen.

Watching her go, I was feeling similarly earnest emotions. *Sorry to your future sister-in-law, but I want to keep you as* my *little sister for a little while longer.*

X   X   X

While I was waiting for the water to boil in the kitchen, I watched my big brother, who was in the *kotatsu* playing with the kitty.

I'd brought up several different options, but I wasn't actually all that worried, in Komachi terms. When you've been observing him at close range for a whole fifteen years, you will find some decently good things about him—even if he really is kind of garbage—and you kinda think maybe someone great might notice those things, too.

Someone who will pull him up from above, or push him up from below, or be involved with him in some other way...

Komachi doesn't know what form that might take, but I've got the feeling someone's gonna take his hand either way.

Until that day, Komachi will continue to look for a (provisional) sister-in-law.

And then the **festival** ends, and a new **festival** begins.

A *fest*.

What do you imagine when you hear that term?

The general interpretation is that when you say *fest*, it's short for the English term *rock festival* and refers to a music event where hollering, partying extroverts gather to not just go all night, but, worst case, party for days.

With booze in one hand, they'll headbang, mosh, stage dive, or sling arms over shoulders for a chicken fight, or get on a portable shrine and call out *wasshoi, wasshoi* like Mirai Moriyama in *Moteki*, to connect through music, even with total strangers, and have an exciting time and share an experience they would surely be unable to forget—that has to be what people imagine is a "fest."

That's about what I imagine, personally. I'll acknowledge my impression is somewhat biased and prejudiced.

But it's not necessarily a bad one. Joining together with others through music and having a good time is actually a great way to enjoy yourself, and I would also say it's one facet of a fest's purpose.

When you get down to it, a *festival* is the same as *matsuri* in Japanese. It's a public occasion.

As they used to say way back when:

Chiba is famous for festivals and dancing. There are idiots who dance and idiots who watch, so if you're an idiot like the rest, you've got to dance and sing a song.

A wise saying. Truly a wise saying. It's so wise, I'm gonna get Megu-Megu-Megurin-Megurisshed☆.

I won't reject that means of enjoyment.

If you read about history, you find that in any era, festivals are a sort of release from constraint, where everyone has permission to indulge. You don't even have to dive all the way into ancient history; it's said that in the banquets following the traditional Shinto rituals starting in the middle ages, everyone regardless of status would drink until they puked… Wait. That's not permissive at all, is it? These days, that's called alcohol harassment, and pulling that even once is in violation of workplace standards.

Modern fests, however, demand a new measure of permissiveness.

That is, namely, giving everyone permission to enjoy themselves in their own way.

Some people like to be a part of a big group that gets all worked up, while others like to privately bask in the music. Therefore, it should be valid to enjoy a fest without yelling, just feeling the vibrations welling up inside you as you remain silent and alone in the venue.

Of course, it's not only fests that have a wide variety of acceptable ways to enjoy them. You could say that's the same for just about all content—movies, music, anime, novels, manga, stage plays, *Mewkledreamy*, and everything else.

Of these, however, fests are exceptional, and I argue that should be recognized.

Judging content by type instead of quality is incredibly foolish, but if you are to make a distinction between a fest and other content, then I'm forced to say that line is drawn by its transient experience.

Movies, anime, and other recorded content are replayable. Being able to watch it many times over if you want to see the same thing is a major plus, but you can't re-create an original experience or the initial impulse of the moment.

Of course, then you can argue that fests and live concerts can be recorded to enjoy a different way a second or third time—and I am compelled to heartily agree. And of course, you can also watch the same movie repeatedly, bragging about the number of times you've watched it to assert dominance within a community.

But it's also inarguable that your very first encounter with that media is unique. There's a certain impact that can only be felt when you come in contact with something for the first time.

That inimitable moment is what makes a fest the ultimate experience. The once-in-a-lifetime enthusiasm and atmosphere created by the venue's audience and the performers onstage can only ever be experienced in that moment.

I can understand the joy of sharing that with friends, and I will offer my unstinting approval for that. But it's also wonderful to meet the challenge alone and meditate privately on the preciousness that must be protected at all costs.

At the end of the day, everyone should enjoy it in the way that they please.

Speaking personally, I strongly contest that a solo battle without interruption, where I can yell and wave my penlight all I want, and then get emo-emo on the way back and write up a concert report as a poem, is all a part of the true pleasure of a fest.

It's fine to go to a fest alone, too. That's what freedom is all about.

Inviting all your neighbors to march with you is also good. Sallying forth alone without any prior arrangements is also good.

So long as you're not causing problems for others, you're allowed to enjoy it in any way you want.

Which means, in other words…

…going to a fest with your little sister should also be allowed.

X   X   X

Another new spring was here.

After somehow squeaking through that reckless, thoughtless, and relentless joint prom with about a hundred yards of elbow grease, a hundred yards of talking, and a few inches of sweet talk, it was finally spring break.

Then, before long, the new semester was upon us.

There was only a little bit of the break left, so I was enthusiastic to make effective use of it, thinking, *I'll power-snooze my way through it just like Meng Haoran!* But such wishes were in vain, and Komachi took me out first thing in the morning.

"Bro, hurry, hurry!" she said. "The fest is gonna start!"

"Yeah, yeah…," I grumbled.

With Komachi shoving me and prodding me in the back, we walked from the station.

We were headed to a certain music festival. That was probably why Komachi was going all out that day, dressed up in a punk black leather jacket, a casual T-shirt, damaged jeans, and boots.

This is a completely trivial fact, but just like the old saying that goes "Chiba is famous for festivals and dancing," Chiba is what they call a fest mecca, and a number of famous music festivals are held here. Apparently, we were marching off to one of those.

I was just an escort here, so I didn't really know the details of the event, but Komachi said it was a pretty big concert.

And Komachi's word was validated by all the hollering, extroverted party types on the way to the venue, even though it wasn't open yet.

I see—it really was the right choice for me to escort her…

Fests aren't just filled with fans who are purely there for the music—I've heard through the grapevine that there are also scoundrels who come for pick-up-related ends.

If a tender, young, and pretty girl like Komachi were to dive in there alone, the concertgoers loitering around the venue would chat her up with a chain of disconnected remarks like *Whooo! You're cute, huh? You in school? How old are you? Where d'you live? So, like, d'you have LINE?* and then before you even know it, she's getting asked on a date. And then afterward, they'll keep going with, like, *Do you have a dream?*

Do you know you can get income like royalties? We're having a barbecue later—wanna come? and then she's canvassed straight into an MLM.

I can't have Komachi getting caught up in some weird online salon! That'd be a disaster! I have to protect her and keep her from suddenly going hollow-eyed and contacting every single one of her old classmates!

Burning with this sense of mission, I strolled along the way to the venue.

There was still quite a lot of time before the show started, but the concertgoers were pouring in, and groups of people wearing band T-shirts and uniforms were starting to stand out here and there. It really had that fest feel—this is a common sight in Chiba, in particular around the Makuhari area. Makuhari has a large event hall, a baseball stadium, and a beach, so it's perfect for a variety of events.

I'm sure some people got tricked by the name Makuhari Messe today, as usual, and got off at Makuhari Station... You have to either get off at Kaihin-Makuhari Station or take the bus from Makuhari-Hongo Station..., I thought as we continued on, and then we came to the venue.

It was just slightly past when they'd opened the doors, and the lobby was thronging with crowds. *I'm sure some of these people tasted despair at Makuhari Station...*

With this kind of concert, generally everyone knows that the time right after the doors open is the most crowded.

But though I may not look like it, I'm rather practiced when it comes to concerts. When you get to my level, what rarely but often happens is you get to the venue anticipating that the concert start will be pushed back by five minutes, leading to your completely missing the opening act. Whoops, that's no good... The useless terminal *otaku* has the tendency to read too deeply into the schedule situation based on the expressions of the staff listening to their headsets.

But judging from this turnout, we could anticipate even greater crowds inside the venue. I honestly wanted to avoid getting pushed around in a sea of people as we waited forever for the show to start. If I were alone, I would have gotten a Max can first before casually strolling over, but this time, I'd come purely as Komachi's escort. I had to ask what she wanted.

...Well then, what do we do? Go home? I asked her with a look, and she pat-patted my shoulder and urged me on.

"Bro, hurry, hurry! Let's go, let's go!"

Komachi-chan seems quite enthusiastic.

Hmm, okay. Today, Big Brother has come to relax and enjoy the music... I'm more in the mood to stay in the back... It's standing room only, so if you're in the front, the trouble from the back moves forward in a wave, you know? I really don't want to get involved in that...

I considered saying something like that to gently guide her with my apparent expertise, but when I looked into Komachi's sparkling little eyes, I couldn't bring myself to say anything so boorish.

As a result, I wound up being really vague. "Like, okay. It's not time for it to start, right? Don't we have some more time?"

Komachi pouted and wagged her finger at me like, *No, no.* "What're you talking about? The fest lasts until you get home, right? Which means...the fest has already started once you've left the house, too!" she declared, puffing out her chest as she pumped a clenched fist into the air. She was so aggressive about it, she won me over by default.

"O-oh. Yeah! That's true! ...I think?" *Is it? Is it true? I agreed automatically, but I feel like that was a pretty irrational argument. Like "If you do it till you win, then you'll never lose!"*

But Komachi thought nothing of her brother's look of skepticism, preparing to barrel ahead. "It is! Never mind—let's just go, let's go! If not, we'll miss hearing the preshow announcement!"

"Y-yeah... Okay, then let's go..."

Aha, so she's the type of *umamusume* who's good at taking the lead from behind? She totally blew right past me at the end. Well, the atmosphere created by the announcer or the narration before a concert starts is part of the live show experience. As expected of my little sister—she's got a sharp eye for these things.

"Let's gooo!" She scampered off, and when she looked back at me, I trotted on after her.

× × ×

When we got into the venue, it was filled with noise.

I could hear expectant whispers, loud and excited chattering, and unfettered yelling. Even in the dark with all the lights off, you could sense the anticipation.

It wasn't long before the show began and the excitement in the hall came to a head. Heck, people were yelling and waving their penlights at the promotional video playing on the big screen.

The front was dominated by hard-core fans of the participating artists and idols, so we automatically took up position in the rear. But you get the best view of the overall buzz of a concert hall from the back. I wasn't really interested in the show to begin with, but standing in the middle of the audience got even me excited.

Eventually, the background music of the hall slowly faded out, and the video on the screen disappeared, too. In inverse proportion, the expectant yelling got even louder.

It was just about to start.

Standard protocol for a concert would be for the general notices to come next. Depending on the show, they might gear it toward the event itself, like having the CEO or the staff make announcements for the producers.

Well then, I wonder what general notices this fest will have, I thought, listening for the announcement.

Then, mingled in the murmuring behind us were some familiar voices.

"So this is the venue for the fest today…"

"We've gotta hurry, or it'll start without us!"

"Of course! Let's go, go, go!"

I heard a particularly composed voice offering commentary, then suddenly a cheerful voice urging her on, followed by a cunning yet charming voice.

But then the first one kept the others from rushing in. "Wait right there. Don't run in the venue. Also…they're about to make the general announcements, so be sure to listen."

"Absolutely!"

"Whoa, she's reeeally into this…"

I overheard an energetic response and a weirded-out reaction, and following a light clearing of the throat, the composed voice continued dispassionately, "'During the performance, either set your cell phones to silent or turn them off. Photos and video and audio recordings are also forbidden. Those who engage in this behavior and fail to heed warnings by staff will be asked to leave the venue, and the event may be interrupted, so we please ask for your cooperation. Furthermore, please be aware that this event is being recorded for video.' That's what it says; do you two understand?" The composed tone went on at length with what sounded rather like the general notices.

"Yep, yep! Follow the rules and enjoy the fest!" the cheerful voice replied brightly, but I had a sneaking suspicion she didn't really get it. That was followed by a quiet, resigned-sounding sigh.

The voices and the conversation sounded so familiar, it made me wonder, *Do I know them?* Though I turned halfway back to get a look, the crowd blocked my view, and I couldn't quite see.

But even within the throng, that cunning-cute voice, the cheerful and cute laugh, and that calm, beautiful tone reached my ears with near-perfect clarity.

"…Then let's have some fun!"

"Whoooo!"

"…Oh, it's about to begin."

I looked toward the front of the venue to see fog wafting up from the stage and a spotlight jumping around.

Finally, the festival begins…

$$\times \quad \times \quad \times$$

It was one big artist after another right from the start, and the fest was in a whirl of excitement.

Though the headliner wasn't out yet, the audience was wild and excited, and their enthusiasm got to me. Before I knew it, I was yelling with my arms up and swinging around a mini-towel. Komachi was also super-busy jumping and hopping around, and time passed in the blink of an eye.

But being in such a big crowd for this long really was exhausting, so when we headed to the washroom, I accepted Komachi's proposal to take a little break as well.

"Ahhh, this is so fun…," Komachi murmured, satisfaction and a comfortable tiredness clear in her voice. I nodded at her as we left the performance hall.

This fest was a pretty long one, so they had a few food stalls set up and a rest area stocked with drinks.

I was feeling a little wobbly from the ringing in my ears and the bass rumbling in the pit of my stomach, so I headed for the rest area.

There, we found a large crowd also recovering their energy for the second half of the battle. Given the size of the event, even the areas outside the performance hall were packed. I pushed my way through the waves of people until I got to the corner by the wall, where I let out a sigh.

Then suddenly, a familiar voice came from behind me. "Ahhh, this is so fun, huh?! The whole audience is really worked up!"

"Right? Too worked up, actually, so I need a break for a moment…"

"Y-yes… Agh…"

It seemed like three girlfriends had come to the fest together.

One of them seemed unused to these sorts of events, as her sigh sounded particularly exhausted and was followed by a remark of concern I could just barely hear. "Oh, you seem pretty tired, Yukinon…" I thought I could hear a little smile as she said a name I was very familiar with. The only Yukinons I know are the Yukino Yukinoshita at our high school and Yukino Bijin from Tracen Academy.

I turned back automatically to look toward the voices.

Komachi had apparently noticed as well, as she called out clearly, "Ohhh! Yui, Yukino!" and an energetic voice replied.

"Komachi, yahallooo! Oh, and yahallo to you, too, Hikki!"

"Oh, Hikigaya."

One of these people was the type you'd expect to find at a fest, and the other was very much not. In other words, it was Yui Yuigahama, waving with lots of energy, and Yukino Yukinoshita, a little pale-faced as she quietly muttered my name. Iroha Isshiki was also with them.

The trio must have decided to wear matching outfits for the event, as they were all in fairly punkish attire: loose, oversized T-shirts with black leather jackets on top and damaged jeans and high-cut boots on the bottom.

Yukinoshita usually came off as modest and feminine, Yuigahama wore a lot of popular, casual clothing, and Isshiki wore a lot of cutesy, soft-and-flowy stuff, so they all had a pretty different charm that day.

"Oh…" I nodded back. The gesture was half out of surprise, like *Funny meeting you here*, while the other half was just confirming it was who I thought it was.

"Oh, it's you." Isshiki responded with a casual bow before giving a questioning look to Komachi beside me. "…And Okome-chan."

Komachi scrunched her face up at that form of address. "Hmm… That sketchy nickname is starting to stick…" She immediately started hopping around, saying her own name again. "It's Komachi! Komachi's name is Komachi!"

With a pat on top of Komachi's head as if to hold her down, Isshiki grinned. "Come on, what's the problem? It's, like, a cute nickname, right? Don't you know that being the younger-girl character who gets teased has its benefits ☆?"

"Ugh, she really is kinda messed up…" Komachi jerked away in horror.

For some reason, Isshiki also had a look of horror. "I mean, he's the one who said that."

"Ugh, it totally sounds like something he'd say..." Then both of them looked at me with contempt.

I didn't say that... I didn't say that at all... False accusation after false accusation...

But this was to break the ice between the two of them, so I would resign myself and accept it.

Isshiki and Komachi had only met each other very briefly during the joint prom, and they hadn't known each other for very long. The fastest way to get them to warm up to each other was to use some mutual acquaintance. Talking dirty behind someone else's back to generate a sense of complicity is the real secret to making friends!

Well, this is Komachi, so I'm sure she'll pull that off with aplomb.

Komachi does have impressive communication skills, if I may say so of my own sister, and has no problem talking openly about all sorts of topics even on first meeting someone or with people older than her. When we went to Chiba Village a while back during summer vacation, she'd managed to communicate well even when everyone else was older than her. She'd also chatted in a friendly way with Kawa-something's little sister, Keika Kawasaki. She can get close to anyone without any prejudice. As expected of the little sister of the world.

That very moment, Komachi was zooming right past me to jump into a conversation with the others.

"I'm glad we could meet up with you, Komachi-chan!" Yuigahama said, waving her hands wide with a smile.

Komachi clapped as well with a gleeful laugh. "No, no, Komachi's glad that you reached out!"

Huh. I see. I'd thought it was an eerie coincidence to just bump into them at a fest at such a large venue, but from the way these two were talking, they'd actually planned this. *Now that I think of it, Komachi was the one to say we should go outside for a break. So that was her excuse, and meeting up like this was the real goal, huh…?* Or so I nearly thought, but hold on a minute here.

"Huh? I wasn't invited." *Why? Why did they skip over Hikki and invite Komachi instead?*

Yuigahama answered a bit hesitantly. "If we told you, you'd say no…"

"Well, that's true…" Even if they had talked to me about it, it would have immediately activated my instakill: "I'll go if I can." And even if I did plan to go, there's a thought pattern common among losers where you gradually become more unwilling to do it as the day gets closer—that's the kind of person I am. It's like whenever you decide on a plan beforehand, it kind of becomes a hassle; what's up with that?

But Komachi is the kind of little sister who will completely understand that temperament of mine. "And that's why Komachi was the one to get the invitation," she said with a smug look and double peace signs.

I'd expect no less… She's got a good grasp on my quirks, knowing that I generally would be unable to refuse a request from my little sister, if it was forced through on zero notice the day of the event. Well, not just Komachi; Yuigahama had to also understand that well, too. That was exactly why she'd chosen to go through Komachi.

Oh no, that's kinda embarrassing… How are they actually this informed about my mode of life? This is embarrassing; I got completely lured out.

I cleared my throat with a *gefum, gefum* and decided to turn the discussion in a different direction. "Huh? If you're gonna say that, then isn't Yukinoshita the same? She doesn't seem like the type to go to events like this…"

When I looked at her, Yukinoshita's weary affect and attention-grabbing classy aura just made my point for me. She stood out so much, it was clear she was unused to this.

A faint smile crossed her face, and she touched a hand to her forehead and looked down. "Y-yes. This is my first time coming here as well… Fests are…wild, aren't they? Ah, hold on, I can't even; I feel weak…"

"Yukino! You're sounding like an *otaku* Twitter account post-concert!" Komachi jumped in with a comeback.

But indeed. She was talking like one of those female *otaku* out there live-tweeting *Wait, I can't even, I'm weak, GoYuu are basically already together…* while she watches anime.

"Regardless, I'm tired…," Yukinoshita said.

Well, she was lacking endurance to begin with. And being in an unfamiliar place like this only had to exacerbate that. That's no surprise if you get hit all of a sudden by the enthusiasm of the crowds. When you're surrounded by so many people, even just standing there is surprisingly exhausting. Getting pushed around by excited concertgoers makes you tired like riding a packed train at rush hour.

"Are you okay? Need a drink or something…?" I asked, just in case.

But Isshiki cut me off. "Oh, you don't have to worry about that. It'll arrive soon."

"Arrive?"

It'll arrive? What's with that completely vague subject? Did you order something on, like, Uber or something? These days, everything is so convenient…, I was wondering, when in the distance, from the edge of the rest area, a familiar someone was laboring his way toward us.

"Dude. The shops were craaazy crowded. I could barely get any drinks at all. This fest is like, whoa."

And there was Tobe, carrying a bunch of drinks in both arms, looking triumphant as he pushed his way over to us. Then when he noticed me, he raised the drinks in both his hands and raced over. "Whoa, huh? It's Hikitani!"

"H-hey… No way, it was Tober Eats…?" I gave Isshiki a look saying, *So you're using the newest delivery service?*

"Act now, and handling fee included, it's basically free," she said blithely.

"Pay him, please…" *He is basically your senior.*

Pretty harsh to send someone older to get drinks, you know... And not getting paid money is exploitation, you know... And it's indescribably cruel to add that he's basically free, you know...

This casual, dirty exploitation tore a cry of anguish from my throat, but it seemed the one being exploited wasn't really bothered.

"Nah, nah, nah, we're cool, we're cool. Here's your drinks." Apparently totally used to this, Tobe started handing out the drinks he'd just bought.

"Thaaanks!" Yuigahama said with her usual level of energy, while Yukinoshita thanked him in a rather tired-sounding voice.

"Thank you..."

"Thanks so much!" Even Komachi was nonchalantly handed a drink in the process.

Meanwhile, Isshiki just thanked him with a very quiet "Mm-hmm."

And so the four drinks Tobe carried in hand were all smoothly sold out. *Hmm... It seems now there's nothing left at all for our friend Tobe...*

"Sorry, I'll pay for Komachi's drink," I said quietly to him. Even if Tober Eats was a functionally free delivery service, Komachi had joined the others just now, so she wouldn't have been in his original count.

"Nah, nah, we're good. You don't hafta...," Tobe answered casually in that who-knows-where-it's-from accent, not seeming bothered at all as he cackled and waved his hands.

The hell, is he a good guy or what...? I was thinking when Tobe finally noticed Komachi's presence.

He gave a melodramatic "Whoaaa!" of surprise, snapped his fingers, and pointed at her. "Wait, you're, like, Hikitani's little sister! Dude! You're basically, like, Sistertani-chan! I haven't seen you in forever! Hey, hey, what's up, whassup? What's goin' on? Oh dude, we gotta catch up. We'll have, like, piles of things to talk about, am I right?"

"Ohhh! It's been a long time! It really has been a long time! We have *so* many things to talk about next time absolutely absolutely honestly we have to later!" Meanwhile, even though Komachi had a wide and bright smile on her face, when Tobe scooted toward her, she backed up a step.

She was even answering him with the kind of expressions you use after everyone's been out drinking together and you're about to leave.

Her skillful snapback made Yuigahama and me jerk away in horror.

"That's how you push someone away when you have no intention of ever talking to them…," I said.

"That thing girls who aren't friends like to do!" Yuigahama cried.

Next time, absolutely, later. In this case, *next time* and *later* will absolutely never come. I'm very informed on this matter.

"Wait, why are you here, Tobe?" I asked. I could basically get Yukinoshita, Yuigahama, and Isshiki being together. But adding Tobe to that didn't really make sense.

"I invited Hayama, but for some reason, this guy just showed up instead," Isshiki answered in an utterly emotionless tone, and Yukinoshita concurred with an equal lack of emotion.

"Indeed. He just showed up."

Ohhh, looks like Miss Yukinoshita's energized now! She's gotten her cutting edge back! Nice, nice!

As for Tobe, on the other hand—you would expect him to cut loose and snap back after that, but there was nothing at all cutting about him. As if he wanted to tell us, *I'd be impressed if you did get me mad*, he chuckled a wry *na-ha-ha*. "Hey, hey, I just came 'cause, like, Hayato told me he'd be worried if the girls went alone."

"Hmm…" I made skeptical noises.

"I mean? Me too, though? Like harassment from dudes and stuff? I wouldn't let that happen?" Though nobody had really asked him, Tobe ruffled up his hair and started to put on a weird show of what a good guy he was. Leave him like this, and he might grow up to be the kind of adult who tries to look cool by tweeting things that everyone will have a hard time reacting to, like *I might look like a troublemaker, but when I saw a young kid drop a can on the ground, I picked it up and tossed it.* Well, Tobe is a good guy…

When everyone there was unable to react, Isshiki let out a deep *aaagh*. "Yeah, he was *reeeally* going on about that… I should've just sent

him a LINE rather than talking to him when I was at the soccer club."
Then she gave Tobe an ice-cold look. "You don't have to show off so
much—drop it. You really should stop doing stuff like that, okay?"

"O-okay... Dude... She's actually lecturing me..." Tugging at the
hair at the nape of his neck, Tobe kept muttering, "Dude...dude."

The way Isshiki was saying it was pretty, uh, *yeah*, but she was
replying to him instead of ignoring him, which made me think she was
actually being fairly nice.

I get it now; I see basically what happened. Probably, when Isshiki
had shown up at the soccer club, she'd mentioned the fest to Hayama,
saying something like *I'll feel anxious if it's just us girls...* And then good
ol' Hayama had used that against her, putting on a charming smile and
carelessly commenting that they could count on Tobe. He is *really* good
at that sort of thing. Saying that in Tobe's presence would also flatter his
pride and chivalrous spirit, which is what brought us to now... In this
world, the nicer you are, the more you get used...

As I was keenly feeling this fact, Yuigahama felt bad for Tobe (of
course) and came in to defend him. "H-hey, now. It is something to be
thankful for..."

Pacified by that highly dubious remark, Isshiki also reluctantly
agreed. "Well, sure, true, I guess..."

Hmm, the way you put it is kinda sketchy, Gahama-chan! ☆

Komachi immediately jumped in then to butter him up. "For
sure! I'm thankful! Hey! Mr. Reliable! Thanks for the drink!" While
she was at it, she tried to get out of paying for the drink she'd just
gotten, too.

*Uh, Big Bro will make sure to pay for that, okay? Come on, that's just
mean.*

As guilt was rising within me, Yukinoshita was starting to smile
with exasperation. It was like she'd been waiting for an opening to
strike. "If a certain someone would have just come from the start, there
wouldn't have been the need for Tobe to get hurt for no reason."

"You were just hurting him, too, though?" *Have you forgotten? You were just treating him like he wasn't invited? And thanks to that, now I'm feeling like I have to apologize for you, too?*

Like a parent apologizing for their problem children, I bobbed a little bow at Tobe. "Well, sorry for making you go along with us."

"Nah, nah, it's no biggie at all, man! ...I totally love being surrounded by sound, too, y'know?" he said, acting super-self-satisfied.

"Ah, I see... All right, then..." I felt like I'd wasted my energy apologizing to him, but just this once, I would let him act cool with that look on his face. He had actually seemed to have fun during the prom, so I'm sure he does enjoy events like this.

"Well, you do seem like you'd be into this stuff," I said, which basically implied, *But the rest of you don't really, right?*

Isshiki picked up on that and quickly replied, "Oh, no, I just thought this would be a good reference for future events. Well, this one is on a way bigger scale, so yeah. But Chiba has some great music festivals, right?"

"Ahhh, true. They do have some really big events," Yuigahama said, nodding a few times, and she was quite right. Chiba actually does have large concerts pretty frequently.

"Ahhh... Like that—that one thing." I nodded along as well and brought up the name of the most famous large-scale event in Chiba's musical history. "...Like the Glay two-hundred-thousand-person concert."

"That's, like, another era?! How old are you, Hikki...?" Yuigahama was aghast.

Don't be stupid; legends surpass eras. That was the event that made the people of Chiba prefecture aware of large-scale music events (personally researched).

Or so I seriously considered arguing back at her, but before I could, Yuigahama shrugged in exasperation. "If you're talking about fests in Chiba, normally you'd bring up Summer Sonic. Or Countdown Japan."

"Well, I'm not very interested in that stuff, so I don't really know..."

"Whaaat? How can you not know them when they're that

famous…?" Isshiki offered her opinion, seeming a bit annoyed, or maybe shocked.

There was even a hint of pity in her dumbfounded expression, and I hurriedly shot back, "Hey, I do know about them. I do, okay…? Well, just the names, and I've never actually gone. Living in the neighborhood actually makes it harder to find the time to go. It's like people who live in Tokyo not going to Tokyo Tower."

Only Tobe responded to my random nonsense with nods of agreement, arms folded. "Yeah, dude, I get that."

Everyone else was looking at me with quite a bit of skepticism. As if she was their representative, Yukinoshita eyed me dubiously and asked, "Do you even go to fests in the first place?"

"Well, that depends on your definition of *fest*…," I said, considering for a while.

The only event I've ever been to that you could properly designate as a fest would be BanNam Fest. *Would Anisama also count? I'm sure you could call it one, in the broad sense of the word… Would Lantis Matsuri count? Hmm, well, I suppose it does. That's a fest.*

Once I'd come to that conclusion, I gave her a big nod. "I go to a lot."

Yuigahama seemed rather surprised. "Huh, that's unexpected. Which ones?"

"I just went to one recently. Two days at Tokyo Dome."

"Two days at Tokyo Dome… Huhhh." Yuigahama sounded impressed, as did Yukinoshita.

"That's quite an amazing artist."

Quite so—Tokyo Dome is one of the major pillars of large music venues in Japan and the pride of the nation. Boasting of a capacity of fifty-five thousand, only the greatest artists can hold concerts there.

Reflecting on that moment, I said, "Well, yeah. Since the second day was *Aikatsu!*…"

That…was…so good…

Man, right from when the narration from Aoi-chan started at the beginning, I had goose bumps. And then after that, the *Aikatsu!* system background music played, right? And also, they call the first song "Daihatsu." And then after that with "Shining Etude," I thought I was gonna die right then and there and find sweet relief. And then when I was ascending to heaven, "Start Dash Sensation" came, and I was falling to my knees somehow even though I was sitting down. Originally, the concept for the second day was an idol festival, but the shared cast there was so incredibly good, I think the way it was put together was nothing short of a miracle. I really felt like I'd gotten a glimpse of the live entertainment of the new era, overcoming the pseudoreligious fervor with which we stan our own personal biases, and it was just *emotional*. Ah, soooo eeeee...eeeemo...

It was such a feelsy vicarious experience, I had degraded into an emotional bot that would endlessly tweet *Emo...emo...e-emo...* One slip, and I would start droning on and on about how good the second day was.

But that's the sort of thing you can write only in a concert report on Twitter, and if you try to do it verbally, your spinal cord will just start saying *emo* without consulting your brain.

As I was eating the emo-emo fruit to become an emo human who could say nothing but *emo, emo*, Komachi was smoothly ignoring that to move the conversation along. "Well, often enough, I suppooose."

"Me too, when I'm going out with friends and stuff," Yuigahama agreed.

"Yeah, dude! For sure!"

"If you mean jazz concerts...," said Yukinoshita. "A long time ago, when my family went on a yacht cruise, there was a concert on the water..."

"Ohhh, the people who can't escape at the end, even when it sinks," said Yuigahama.

"Isn't that the *Titanic*...?" Komachi cut in.

"But I feel like that's not quite the same type of concert," said Isshiki.

"Yes," Yukinoshita agreed. "So I'm not sure how I should enjoy this kind."

"Oh, well, my brother knows a lot about that. Right, Bro?"

"Yeah." With the discussion suddenly turned to me, I instantly suspended my vicarious emo experience and nodded sharply.

"You were listening?!" Yuigahama cried.

"Well, yeah. No matter when it is or what I'm doing, Komachi's voice is the one thing I'll always hear. I'd even say I wasn't listening to anything but Komachi's voice," I said.

Komachi beamed a bright, happy smile. "Wow, that's creepy! ♪" she said cruelly.

And Yukinoshita did not smile; the disgust on her face seemed fairly serious. "That really is creepy…"

Hmm, such direct disparagement strikes me right in the heart, you know… It comes off as such a natural response—not good.

Brought back to reality all at once, I returned to the subject of the conversation while I was at it. Clearing my throat with a *gefum, gefum* to express its importance, I decided to initiate them on how to enjoy concerts. "…So a concert. You don't have to get too complicated about it. At first, you just have to do the M. Bison stance. Like you're the boyfriend."

However, the moment I said that, Yukinoshita's expression twisted in confusion. "M….Bison? What? What did you say?" she asked back.

So I repeated it one more time. "Uh, like I said, M. Bison standing boyfriend face."

"That doesn't explain anything!" Yuigahama wailed, smooshing her bun.

I suppose I shouldn't be surprised that the expression is a bit difficult for an amateur…

I searched anew for words it seemed would get through to them. "…Ah, maybe it'd be easier to get if I said it like that—the old-fashioned-man look."

"I don't get what you mean! Well, I get what the words mean…but I don't get it. Huhhh? Why would you act like you're the boyfriend at a concert…?" Yuigahama was already starting to abandon understanding, *hmm-hmm*ing to herself.

But beside her, Isshiki was nodding. "Oh-ho. Now I'm curious what sort of *intense* look you put on your face while you gloat."

"Wow, she sure doesn't put things gently… Well, but Komachi is curious, too."

"Indeed. Then give it a try, to show us just what it's like," said Yukinoshita.

"Well, it's nothing really difficult… Um, kinda like this…," I said, folding my arms and standing at an angle to gaze into the distance. My eyes were not now or here, but on a metaphysical idol.

Gazing beyond the shining lights to the stage that only I could see, I smiled peacefully and slowly nodded. In my mind, I said, *I understand—I'm the only one who really does. Who understands you. The real you… It's just me…*

Instantly, everything sounded far away.

A painfully awkward silence fell over five people, but despite it all, I was still nodding along.

And then, in my heart, I said to the formless idol in my imagination, *…I see. So you've found…the place you want to be… You're shining so bright… So, so much brighter than before.*

I ruminated on the nonexistent days that idol and I had shared, aware that they were lost in the distant past, sighed in mild self-deprecation, and lightly shook my head.

Gazing into the middle distance with a miserable smile of regret, I answered under my breath, "Yeah. I have a good view of you from the seat at the very back…"

I think Isshiki'd had about enough of this dude, as she shook her head violently. "No way, no way, no way."

Komachi and Yuigahama did the same as if to say, *Not happening.*

"Yikes, yikes, yikes."

"Creepy, creepy, creepy."

"Emo, emo, emo." Only I could see the truth. I chanted *emo, emo*; I would not lose to the great chorus of *no way yikes creepy*.

But it's only me, Bump of Chicken, and people on drugs who try to see things that cannot be seen. Yuigahama, the most relatively wholesome and well-adjusted of us, seemed disturbed. "What's so emotional about that?!"

"You make yourself emotional watching that way, so it's fine."

Yes—at a fest or concert or whatever, the only important thing is whether you get feels or not.

Yukinoshita's discomfort turned into confusion—even concern—after my earnest appeal. "...What's so enjoyable about that?"

She spoke with great consideration, as if touching a sensitive spot, very much like when it's dead silent at the dinner table and your mom screws up her courage to ask, *...Are you having fun at school?*

She looked so uneasy asking me that, I was forced to answer her seriously. "Uh... Of course. It feels good to be the only one not screaming. Putting on the old-fashioned-man look makes you feel like the protagonist of a Makoto Shinkai film. You get theme music in your head and everything."

"Listen to the music in the concert, not the music in your head..." Yukinoshita touched her temple as if she had a headache and breathed an exasperated sigh.

Hmm... So you don't get it, huh...? It feels so good to look down on the screaming masses. You get so many feels.

The moment I feel most connected to my bias is when I can act like I have transcended mere fan-hood to understand her like no one else can. A man such as I can reach an even higher level of enjoyment by drawing such lines of discrimination between myself and other fans in the deepest areas.

But they probably wouldn't get that. Yuigahama's mouth was hanging open. "I don't get it at all... Creepy."

"That's...ew," Isshiki agreed.

Stop taking it so seriously, okay? Like just now, I kinda got the sense you really, truly meant that?

But Yuigahama wasn't the only one with a serious tone. Yukinoshita also seemed concerned. "Do you always do things like that? Are you all right? Are you making sure to take your medicine three times a day?"

"No need. My brain's always in a happy stupor when I'm watching a concert."

"It's not always good to be too happy, I see…" Yukinoshita's gaze was so incredibly gentle. Like the tragic warmth of a caregiver nursing an invalid.

The mood was starting to feel like someone died. Isshiki sighed in utter exasperation. "Isn't there a more straightforward way to enjoy a concert?" she said, sounding incredibly fed up. Her expression said that it would feel too viscerally awkward for her to intrude any further.

But even if she asked for such a thing, I personally saw this as the most straightforward and emotional way to enjoy a fest. Well, she had to be asking me to, like, focus on more mainstream sensibilities. "When you get used to it, you start memorizing the calls and stuff, so you can enjoy it just fine."

"Calls?" This use of the English word must have been unfamiliar to Yukinoshita, as she tilted her head.

Then Tobe nodded like, *Uh-huhhh* and butted in. "Yeah, yeah, yeah, calls are like that thing, right? Like *Vaaanilla Vanilla Vaaanilla whoo whoo* sorta thing?"

"No." Well, he got the rhythm basically right, so yeah, I guess it's close, but it's totally different. You don't see the Vanilla truck around these days, so nobody'll get it… *There is one girl here who's nodding along, but I will pretend I didn't see that.*

"A call is like a sort of interjection in a song," I said, but I still had trouble explaining it.

I could elaborate by saying *Basically, it's that thing where you go "Umapyoi! Umapyoi!" in a winning live,* but I really couldn't expect them to get that. When watching that ending scene, you generally just cry, and it's no time for doing the calls anyway... I never thought the day would come when I would cry from *umapyoi*... Well, leaving that aside.

"Well, to pick a popular one..." I considered it, then picked the most straightforward example that came to mind. "One, two! Yeeeah, yeeeah, yeah yeah yeah! ...Something like that."

Yuigahama and Isshiki nodded. "Ahhh, I kinda feel like I've heard that before...," Yuigahama said.

"That is basically how idol concerts go," Isshiki agreed.

"Ohhh, do you like idols, Iroha?" Komachi asked her.

"Not enough to go to concerts, obviously... But, well, I like pretty girls."

"You really don't put things gently."

As Komachi and Isshiki were discoursing on idols, Yukinoshita was falling into thought. "Hmm... It seems a little strange for the audience to be calling out, when they've come to hear the music."

"Well, it's really about cheering them on. Though you do have to look for cues and check to see if you can do it or not right then..."

Views on fan chants differ depending on the person. Some people see them as an annoyance, while others value them as part of what makes the experience exciting. Of course, some believe that it depends on the song, so this is a matter to be treated with the utmost delicacy. If I may add further, sometimes the management establishes clear rules for it, so it's recommended you look over all the rules when participating."

I could have gone on at length, but there was just one thing that was more important than all of that. "Of course, for a concert, as long as you're not causing trouble for others, you can enjoy yourself in any way you want."

Ultimately, what should be the greatest priority is that the performers and the audience all have a pleasant time. I would even call this the absolute ironclad rule.

My delivery might have been a bit too intense, but that made me sound all the more convincing. Yukinoshita blinked a few times, but then quickly broke into a smile. "I see. I understand now. Somehow." With a sigh of satisfaction, she nodded.

Meanwhile, Isshiki was sighing for other reasons. "But being free to do what you want can be the hardest thing… Agh, seriously, what do we do for this event?" she muttered to herself. I was surprised to hear the concern in her voice, so I considered her question.

Though I said you could enjoy it how you pleased, that's ultimately the mind-set for participating as an audience member. Those managing and planning an event have to see things from a different point of view. Saying "How you enjoy it is up to you!" may sound good, but that's basically throwing everything on the guests. You have to consider how you want them to enjoy themselves, what areas you want them to enjoy, and how you'll give them a good time.

If we looked at this big fest from the management angle, that should offer some hints. For example, this rest area was one element I would very much like them to incorporate, please. It's comfortable to have a place like this at cultural festivals, too… You could even make all the classrooms spots to rest in. Then the classes won't have to do any work at all.

So there were matters of hospitality to consider, but that would come after the content of the event was decided.

"Wait, what kind of event are you planning to have?" I asked.

Isshiki touched her index finger to her jaw, pondering as she began to talk. "I was thiiinking around next spring, it'd be nice if the student council could hold an event celebrating graduation or the school entrance ceremony. Wouldn't it be nice to go all out for something fancy? It's school money anyway, so it's just a waste if we don't use it, riiight?"

"Whoa, what a thing to say… That's the worst reason for planning an event…" Isshiki's rationale was just so out there, Komachi was jerking away in horror.

Isshiki pouted. "*I* don't see a problem. We're a public school; it's tax money. It was my money to begin with."

"It's *our* money...," Yukinoshita said, a little taken aback, while Yuigahama was smiling anxiously.

Only one of us, Tobe, was nodding like, *Yeah, that's Irohasu.* He's used to her, huh?

Leaving that aside, the time of year for the event was also a rather difficult issue. "Hmm... Spring, huh...?" I said. "Well, if you're gonna do it, having it around graduation is best."

"You think?" Isshiki asked.

"Yeah, entrance time isn't great..."

My vague equivocations made Isshiki tilt her head. "Why's that?"

"'Cause that's right when all the new students are most excited and start doing dumb stuff. When you do something dumb in the first few days of school, the effects linger down the line."

The time when you've just entered a new school is the most anxious period in particular. There's nothing more painful than stumbling at the starting line. You're only just stepping into a community, so the friendships that will become your lifelines haven't entirely firmed up, while your attachment to the school itself is still weak. The temporary shame becomes too much, and you speedrun right into withdrawing from school. I'm very informed on the matter.

Perhaps too informed, in fact.

"That's scarily convincing!" Yuigahama was vigorously agreeing.

"Right?" I nodded. "The first self-introductions at a new school are like that, too. It gets real bad when you screw up there."

"Yeah, man, that's a total disaster! It's like, y'know? In the fest just now, that line when they first came onstage? That was a real crisis." Tobe jabbed a finger at me, nodding like he was convinced.

Well, I feel slightly hesitant about likening a big-name artist MCing at a fest to a self-introduction at a new school, but in both cases, the first thing you say is important.

Komachi, as one about to start at our school herself, looked a bit bummed about this talk. "Now Komachi doesn't feel as good about it..." Her expression seemed uneasy.

Yuigahama reacted with surprise. "Really? You seem like you'd be fine, Komachi-chan."

Well, fair enough. When you're a Komachi-class skilled communicator, then basic self-introductions should be a snap... What is she even worried about...?

Confused, I looked at Komachi to see her eyes were all wibbled up as she earnestly appealed to Yuigahama. "No, I'm not sure now! Could you show me an example? In a fest-like way! Just like how those idols in the show did it!"

The sudden wild request made Yuigahama flail in bewilderment. "Huh? Huh?"

Ahaaa, so this was what Komachi was after? She's getting swept away in the excitement of the fest...

So I was thinking, but Isshiki also smirked. "Oh, I like that. Then introduce yourself, please."

Yukinoshita put a hand to her lips and tittered. "Yes, you seem like you'd be good at that sort of thing. Why not do it for her?"

Meanwhile, Tobe was clapping his hands like, *Yeah, c'mon*, too, making it harder and harder for her to refuse.

"Huhhh... U-um, okay... Something fest-worthy, like those idols in the show..." Yuigahama's eyebrows came together, and she closed her eyes, *hmm*ing as she considered something. From her muttering, it seemed she was trying to recall how the idols who'd just been onstage had introduced themselves.

Eventually, the image must have come together in her mind, as her eyes flashed open, and she put on a sparkling smile. And then with large, enthusiastic gestures, she called out, "Yahallo, everyone! All you guys say it, too! Yahallooo!" Then she cupped her hands around her ears and waited for a response.

If she was gonna wait like that, then we were forced to reply. When she did get some proper calls of "Yahallooo," she nodded in satisfaction and waved her hands. "Okay, everyone, thanks! This is the aaalways cute, sometimes sexy, all-pink: Yuipon! I'm in charge of greetings!" She put her hands to her cheeks cutely and then her hands on her hips sexily, then spun her hands around into a sharp salute. They were pointlessly flawless idol gestures.

"Ohhh, whoa, she's actually doing it." Her arrogant manner aside, Isshiki was applauding.

Then that was followed by a thick-voiced cheer and an awfully deep voice.

"Whoaaa! Queeeen!"

"Yuipoooon!"

"Two *otaku* have entered the chat…"

The reactions from the two *otaku*…er, Tobe and Komachi were so on point, Isshiki was physically recoiling. Especially from Komachi, who had her face smooshed up as she called out in a deep voice.

Isshiki turned back to glance at me like, *Aren't these two kinda ugh?* But I was well beyond that.

"…Huh? Huh? Wait, huh, I can't, I'm ded lol. I can't even, too cute…," I muttered in spite of myself in a near-inaudible whisper. "Huh, huh, wait. What just happened? Wait, I can't. Huh? I could just, like, fall to the ground at any minute. Yeah, yeah, this is it—the people who come to idol shows, this is what they're coming for. I could stan Yuipon for real." I rambled on and on at ultra-high speed as Isshiki eyed me with utter disgust.

"A third *otaku*…" Isshiki seemed resigned, like *These guys are lost.* She looked to Yukinoshita for help.

"Rather than 'in charge of greetings,' 'in charge of yahallo' would be better."

"And then over here is the producer…"

But Isshiki's hopes were in vain, as Yukinoshita was standing there with her arms folded and going full producer, trying to enforce her own vision.

And then Yuigahama was taking her seriously, just like an idol. "Hmm, but *yahallo* is a greeting…"

"Someone you've never met before will sometimes not understand that it's a greeting, won't they? We're used to hearing it, so we get it, but others might assume you're making strange sounds, like an animal cry," explained Yukinoshita.

"That's how you thought of it?!"

"Oh, of course I thought of it as cute chirping. Very cute chirping."

"You suck at backpedaling!"

There was no malice in Yukinoshita's smile, but her backpedaling really did suck... You'd only ever see "Its chirping is cute!" as a selling point for a bird in a pet shop...

Even Isshiki couldn't stand by and watch this anymore; she shrugged as if to say, *Good grief.* "Well, that was pretty mean, Yukino. So why don't you give it a try?" she casually declared.

Yukinoshita froze. "Huh?!"

Looking over, I saw Isshiki's mouth split open with a cruel chuckle.

"Oh, I wanna see it, I wanna see it. Oooh, clap, clap."

"Clap, clap, clap, clap."

Despite Yukinoshita's confusion, Yuigahama and Komachi carried out a wonderful co-op move, applauding as if to say, *I've been waiting for this!*

After joining in on the earlier teasing and playing the producer just now, Yukinoshita couldn't refuse. "Huh, huh? ...F-fest-like? ...Like an idol?" she muttered, holding her head in her hands and groaning.

Come on, guys, this is taking it too far. Don't put Yukinoshita on the spot too much. She can't take this. But I will not say so...since I do kinda wanna see?

With everyone's expectations gathering around her, Yukinoshita hung her head awkwardly and then quickly arranged her bangs. She closed her eyes and let out a little breath, bit by bit getting herself in the mood. Crimson slowly grew on her cheeks until she eventually opened her dewy eyes.

"E-everyone! Good evening! Long black hair is the proof of intellect...and my theme color and heart are blue. I'm Yukinon, in charge of cool..." Following the template of the greeting Yuigahama had pulled off, Yukinoshita swished back her glossy black hair, touching her hand to her chest with a reserved smile. That idol gesture was too cute to be called cool, and it had a touch of passion.

"O-ohhh…"

She wasn't just blushing, but red to her ears as she introduced herself. Silence fell around all of us.

Everyone was speechless, enchanted. Yukinoshita must have taken our silence as a lack of reaction, as her shoulders trembled in distress. And then she gave me a look of teary-eyed resentment, biting the edge of her pouting lip, before weakly hanging her head.

"…I want to die," she muttered, hesitant and hoarse. The childish fragility of her words surprised everyone. I felt a dull stabbing like *Urk!* in my heart.

"Nah, dude, that was great!" Tobe offered her unstinting applause, and Yuigahama squeezed her tight.

"It was supercute! I love it!"

Though Yukinoshita looked bothered about being swept into her embrace, she finally let out a sigh. The relief eased the tension from her expression, and even squirming in embarrassment, she had a bashful smile on her face. "O-oh, really…?"

"Yeah!" said Isshiki. "It even made me think, *Whoa, that lady's on it; that's playin' dirty!*"

"Whoa, you have a strange way of complimenting people. But it was actually cute! Right, Bro?"

But everything sounded so far away—Isshiki's awful remarks and even Komachi addressing me.

When I didn't say anything, Komachi gave me a questioning look. "…Bro?"

But there was nobody to answer her call.

Nothing but a corpse that wouldn't speak as crickets chirped in the distance. Komachi gently shook the shoulder of that corpse.

No reply. It's just a corpse.

"H-he's dead…"

Hachiman Hikigaya. Age at death: seventeen years.

Cause of death: shot through the heart.

"B-Bro!" With that pained cry, Komachi shook my body back and forth.

Thanks to that, I somehow managed to regain consciousness. "…Ah!"

That was close. I just about died there from seeing something too absolutely precious. My grandma and grandpa who're still alive were on this side of the Sanzu River, waving their hands good-bye… They were totally waving me off, huh…?

That really was close. If I die every time over things like this, I'm not gonna have enough lives no matter how many I get, am I? Is my life *Spelunker* or what?

Breathing a sigh of relief, I wiped the sweat off my forehead and pretended like nothing had happened. "…So what were we talking about again?"

Seeing my bewilderment, Isshiki told me with a bit of exasperation, "About introducing yourself at a new school."

I pulled myself together and folded my arms with a *hmm.* "Ahhh, that. With self-introductions of that type, you can't babble on too long. Getting it done quickly is ideal," I expressed eloquently.

Komachi nodded with deep interest. "Oh-ho, I see. So why is that?"

"The reason is extremely simple… Chatty but socially inept is the most irritating type," I said.

Socially inept doesn't refer only to those who can't talk. It can refer to everyone in general with difficulties in communication. Some of the socially inept will talk quite a lot, blabbing on and on when nobody is listening. There are also different subtypes: kids who talk too much simply because they can't read the atmosphere, pretentious gorillas who like to assert dominance and like hearing the sound of their own voice, and also panickers who wind up babbling when they get nervous.

Compared with those chatty socially inept types, a radio that's breaking down and you can't hear anything from is somewhat preferable... Wait, if you can't hear anything from it, that's not breaking down. Isn't that just broken?

Yukinoshita gave an *mm-hmm* as if my statement very much made sense to her, and then a soft smile rose to her lips. "That's a rather good self-introduction. I think it would be even better if you said your name first next time."

"Thanks for the advice. Does anyone have a mirror?" *Could someone please lend that girl one?*

I looked over to see Yuigahama with an awkward expression as she made an attempt to patch things up. "Um, it's like, you know! You're pretty much kinda like that, too, Yukinon!" she said.

Yukinoshita sulked. *Making cute faces won't get you anywhere. Make sure to reflect on your words, okay? I need to do that, too.*

Anyway, if you're going to talk, then you have to regulate yourself objectively.

If you don't, then later, once your head has cooled and you look back on it, you'll want to die! Ah, now I'm remembering, and it's making me want to die.

My gaze pulled down on its own to land on Komachi's face. She was looking like she found this a little difficult to comprehend. "Mm, I see... So what you choose to talk about is important. But then...Komachi can't really be sure without seeing some specific examples. Glance." And yes, she said *glance* out loud as she looked at me.

I decided to pretend I hadn't heard that, whistling to myself in a deliberate sort of way, but Komachi just kept muttering, "Glance, glance, glance..." And then she tugged on my sleeve, too. "You give it a shot, too, Bro. Look, you can't make just them do it."

"You're the one who made them...," I said.

But Komachi just smiled like *tee-hee-blep* ☆ and clonked herself on the forehead. Maybe she felt guilty for having gotten carried away and for embarrassing Yuigahama and Yukinoshita.

Then shouldn't you do it yourself, huhhhhh? This big bro will do just about anything my little sister asks. *Aw geez! My Komachi-chan is so good at getting what she wants!*

Even as I was thinking this, it was getting harder and harder to say no.

Yukinoshita folded her arms as if to say, *Show me what you've got.* Meanwhile, Yuigahama clapped, Komachi looked at me with sparkling eyes, and Tobe was saying "Dude, dude."

As if coordinating the whole group, Isshiki cleared her throat and gestured to me. "Well then, introduction, please."

"Uhhh, okay."

Yuigahama and Yukinoshita had gone through such great hardships; I had to do it, too. But wasn't Miss Gahama actually pretty into it? Eh, whatever.

I would soon be in my third year of high school. If I included my elementary school years, there had been about a total of ten opportunities for me to introduce myself for a new school year. Basing this on experience, I can say 80 percent of self-introduction failures are caused by overeagerness.

It's important not to try (and fail) to be funny, but not be too apathetic, either—to talk about yourself plainly, as you are.

And so after going through my metaphysical entrance ceremony and facing my metaphysical classmates for the first time, I made my sensible self-introduction.

"My name is Hachiman Hikigaya."

"That's kinda like an introduction a main character would give..." Isshiki gave me a skeptical look.

"The sort of normal high school boy you'd see anywhere."

"A protagonist..." Yukinoshita's brows drew together. "Completely ordinary, living a boring but peaceful life every day."

"That's a main character..." My fake self-intro made Yuigahama smile wryly.

"...But then one day I suddenly meet the mysterious fairy Loneron, and suddenly on the first day of school, I become a loner! What's gonna happen to me now?!" I cried.

"Wait, is this PreCure?!" Yuigahama cried, jerking away in part surprise, part exasperation, and part distress, with double the feeling.

Uh, that's just how self-intros are. That's what they always do in the scene before the OP, right?

But I didn't have the time to explain that before Isshiki waved her hands in front of her chest as if to say, *No way, no way.* "Come on, you didn't need the bit about the mysterious fairy there."

Yukinoshita also added with a smile, "The question isn't what's going to happen—it's what's already happened to his head."

"Harsh!"

As Miss Gahama said, their grading was pretty severe. Even Tobe was taken aback like, "Dude…"

Meanwhile, the one who'd dumped this nonsense on me seemed quite satisfied with herself. "Mm-hmm. Your intro was frankly pretty *eh*, but it's useful for reference! Komachi has the feeling school will work out somehow!" she said as she pumped her fist in a triumphant pose.

Oh-hooo, verily sooo? I'm terribly concerned as to what part of that self-intro will be useful to her, and how.

Komachi, however, ignored my unease and contemplated her new beginning. "Finally, Komachi will be going to school with Yukino and Yui. Komachi's really looking forward to it!"

"Me too!"

"Yes, we'll be waiting for you at school."

Watching the three of them together chattering like that, Isshiki made a noise like *mggg* as she watched. "Ngk… My position as youngest…" Isshiki gritted her teeth. Apparently, she had some very particular concerns.

Tobe attempted to console her. "C'mon, dude, it's a good thing to have someone younger around. It's like…having people rely on me gets me motivated? I just always end up indulging 'em. Like treating them to food and stuff." He was fully playing the reliable elder as he proudly mussed the hair at the back of his head.

But when you're as approachable as Tobe is, I'm sure that does help the younger kids in a lot of ways. He might actually be a really dependable senior.

So I was thinking, but it seems not so! Isshiki cut him right down with a chilly gaze and a low tone. "Agh, well, that's just people sending you on errands 'cause they have no respect for you."

Tobe instantly froze. "Huh? For real?"

"For real."

"...Dude..." Tobe didn't say anything to that sharp and cutting truth from Isshiki. All he could do was muss at his collar.

U-um, hey, I think that's one of the things that makes you a good senior... If you weren't, then Irohasu wouldn't be able to be so brutally honest. I think that might mean she's just opened her heart to you that much...

When I was hesitating as to whether I should try to be supportive and say that, suddenly Komachi spun to face me. Then she gave Isshiki a cutesy grin. "Eh-heh, please take care of me. ♪"

It was so sudden, Isshiki's expression went blank. She blinked a couple of times, then cleared her throat quietly. "Hrm... Well, maybe it's not bad to have someone younger around," she said as she looked away. It seemed she was flattered by the prospect of someone looking up to her. I cracked a crooked smile as she quietly finger-combed some of her hair over her ears.

"So watch out for her, if anything happens," I said.

Isshiki and Komachi would be together a year longer than the rest of us, with our graduation waiting in the spring. *Such a connection with an older girl should be encouraging...*, I thought, nodding with my arms folded like an old kung fu master.

Isshiki gave me a skeptical look. "Agh, you can ask me for whatever, but there isn't much I can d—" Then she must have realized something, as she cut off there. She jerked backward, flapping her hands hastily as she rattled off quickly, "Ah! Were you just hitting on me, 'cause like it's not so bad if you're casually proposing and implying like 'please take care of my little sister,' but now that I think about it being youngest is the juiciest position so I'm sorry." Then she bobbed her head in a clean bow.

Satisfied by that, I nodded a couple of times. "Yeah, sure."

Isshiki would come up with these nonsense reasons to reject me in seconds over every little thing, completely unprompted. It had enabled me to ignore it from the start.

But Isshiki seemed unsatisfied, as she was puffing up her cheeks sulkily and pouting. "There it is—you're not listening again…"

"It'd be crazier to actually listen to something like that… I did give you an answer, like *Yeah, sure*." At this point, it's just a basic conversational flow task; topics roll up on the conveyor belt in front of me, and I plop little dandelions like *I get that* and *For sure* on top of them. Though it's trash labor that doesn't pay.

But those thoughts must have been totally obvious, as Isshiki breathed a resigned sigh. "Well, I suppose that's true…"

"Yeah, yeah, for sure," I agreed carelessly, and Komachi made an *oh-hooo* sound like she was somehow super-impressed. There was a sparkle in her eyes as she watched Isshiki and me.

Then Komachi timidly addressed Isshiki. "Ummm…"

"Yes? What is it, Okome-chan?" Isshiki said with a long-suffering sigh.

Komachi clasped her hands together in a praying gesture and said sweetly, with wibbly eyes, "Could I call you 'big sister'? I could even start with 'provisional' and then go from there on a case-by-case basis?"

"Why?! I don't wanna! That assessment seems like a huge hassle!" Isshiki refused flatly.

But Komachi ignored her so hard, it was refreshing. "In ancient times, people said: an eye for an eye, a tooth for a tooth, and trash for trash… You're the best option, according to that old adage. If nothing else, In a sense, you're actually the ideal big sister—in a sense."

"Huh? What the heck is she talking about…? And that doesn't feel like a compliment at all..." Isshiki eyed my spellbound and dreamy sister distrustfully. Her nose was wrinkled in the classic expression of being weirded out.

But Komachi completely ignored that, too. "You know, Komachi doesn't need a brother at all times, so I was thinking I'd like a big sister...since that would ultimately be best for him... My concern is worth a lot of Komachi points."

"Oh? It is? But you said you don't need a brother, so doesn't that mean it scores pretty low?" I shot back. *The debt you incurred on the first half was so big, you can't repay it on the latter half anymore, can you? You should reconsider where you're allotting your points, okay?* But it seems that point allotment is highly subjective.

Unexpectedly, Yuigahama and Yukinoshita started muttering to themselves. "Komachi-chan as a little sister...might be nice."

"Me as a big sister... That's not so bad."

When they noticed they'd spoken at the same time, they looked at each other. "Huh?"

"Oh?"

They stared at each other wordlessly—one smiling boldly, one smiling arrogantly. Somehow that brief confrontation felt very, very long.

"Whoa, this is definitely gonna be a hassle...," Isshiki muttered quietly in the perilous air that hung around them.

Even Tobe was mussing the hair at the back of his head as he scrambled for an excuse. "Dude... Ah! The artist I came for is coming soon; gotta go!" Before he'd even finished his sentence, he scampered off as fast as he could.

Isshiki yelled after him. "Ah, hey! Why're you running away?!"

"Dude!" Tobe cried over his shoulder as he ran. His escape speed and his crisis-detection abilities were excellent—he was moving like the comic relief character who would survive to the end in a Hollywood movie.

Isshiki let out a loud "Agh," then clapped her hands to get herself back in the mood. "Okay! We can talk more about this next time! So let's wrap this up, too!" she said with extra cheer, cutting in between Yukinoshita and Yuigahama. The fest was approaching the latter half. This would be the perfect time to end our break.

I went wholeheartedly in on Isshiki's suggestion. "Y-yeah. It's that time anyway," I said, and Yuigahama and Yukinoshita glanced over at the clock. Then they looked at each other again and exchanged warm smiles.

The tension relaxed all at once, and Yuigahama stretched wide. "Yeah! We're almost at the climax of the fest after all!"

"...Well then, let's enjoy the second half as much as the first," Yukinoshita said with a calm smile.

"Whoo!" Komachi thrust a fist high.

With that as our signal, we left the rest area and started heading back to the hall.

Perhaps it was thanks to a full break, or perhaps their hearts were racing in anticipation of the climax of the fest, but the girls' steps were buoyant.

The lights spilling out from the performance hall hit their silhouettes walking a few steps ahead of me, and it was so bright, it made me squint.

Their long shadows did not stay in one place, wavering back and forth, fuzzy and fading into their surroundings, but they were clearly overlapping.

The moment I saw that, my feet stopped—I'd uncharacteristically found myself wanting to look at them a little longer.

"Hikigaya, what are you doing? We'll leave you behind." Yukinoshita turned to question my pause, while beside her, Yuigahama was waving her arms wide.

"Hikki, hurry, hurry!"

"You're too sloooow." Isshiki was aggressively sullen.

"Big Bro, let's go, let's go!" Komachi hopped up and down, beckoning to me.

How many more times would I get to see them all lined up together?

There was only a little time left. Eventually, the seasons would pass, and a fleeting parting awaited us when spring visited once more.

The festival time would not last forever, either. That inevitable end is what makes a festival a festival.

Turn it the other way, and you can say that all things that end eventually are festivals.

So then—

—even these days of nothing are a kind of festival.

They are our fest.

I'm sure they're singular occurrences, things that happen only once in a lifetime: unique, ultimate experiences.

Someone long ago once said Chiba is famous for festivals and dancing. There are idiots who dance and idiots who watch, so if you're an idiot like the rest, you've got to dance and sing a song.

It truly is a wise saying.

I chuckled under my breath. "Yeah, I'm coming."

Then I headed to the finale, where the headliner was waiting.

I strode off to the performance hall where I could watch the awesome climax with my own eyes. Where they waited.

Nonchalantly, casually, **Iroha Isshiki** assembles a future.

Cherry blossom petals were piled up in a corner of the courtyard.

It was just past the halfway point of April.

As time shifted, the color of the light filtering through the trees was also changing. With each gust of the gentle, warm breeze, vivid greens waved to the passing season.

Studying the branches where leaves had already replaced blossoms, I pressed a button on the vending machine.

Without even looking at my hands, my fingers automatically reached out for the usual brand of canned coffee. It fell with a clunk.

Can in hand, I wandered over to a bench in the school courtyard.

Nobody else would bother coming outside just for the ten-minute break between classes.

Right now, the courtyard was mine—Hachiman Hikigaya's private space. *Worst case, they might levy a property tax in the name of Hachiman Hikigaya. Seriously, the taxes are too high... Couldn't they at least lower the consumption tax or something?*

The emphasis on my concern for and interest in politics and economics would help with my campaign for Chiba prefectural governor at some point in the future. I squeezed the Max can in my hands.

Life is bitter, so coffee, at least, should be sweet...

About to spoil myself with this sweet pleasure, I was trembling with joy, enshrined with dignity in the center of the bench and feeling increasingly more satisfied with myself—until I heard some gleeful chattering getting closer and closer.

Someone had stepped into my private space. *Come on, man. Who is it? Pay up for the property tax*, I thought as I glanced over questioningly.

A few girls were ambling along the covered walkway. I assume they were returning from a class in a different room—they were chatting in a very lively manner as they headed back to the main school building.

Among these girls, a pale head of hair happened to catch my eye.

Her hair was fluffy and shone in the sunlight, her big, round eyes as charming as a little squirrel's. Her uniform was also worn just a bit casually, and though the way she held the baggy cuffs of her oversized cardigan sleeves was a familiar sight to me, I couldn't help but find it adorable.

Well, she's always adorable—that's just Iroha Isshiki.

I'm so used to how careless and sloppy she acts in the clubroom and student council room, I tend to forget. Seeing her with her friends, it hit me again.

She's actually getting along well in her new class. That's nice, that's nice..., I thought, watching her with avuncular fondness, which might have been too much. She noticed me, and our eyes met for a moment.

Isshiki remained silent, opening her mouth like *Ah*. No, maybe it was *Ugh*.

But the surprise showed on her face for only an instant, and she immediately covered it with a little smile, doing a small wave in front of her chest with her fingers just slightly peeking out from her overlong cardigan sleeves.

That gesture and smile were so sneaky and secretive, like she was doing it so the others couldn't see, like a sign for a lovers' tryst. It was super-embarrassing.

I couldn't figure out how I should respond. All I could do was return an eye signal somewhere between a nod and a bow. As I was busy getting flustered, Isshiki went back to chatting with her friends before vanishing into the main school building.

Once they were gone, I breathed a heavy and listless sigh, then looked up at the sky.

How should I have reacted just now? Did she think I was ignoring her? Should I have waved back? No, that'd be creepy, too. A bow? Should I have bowed? If Isshiki had been alone, that could be an option, but you act a little differently when there are other people around. Or should I have used a fake yawn to just pretend I wasn't looking? Whatever it is, thinking this hard about it really is creepy, huh?! That's not good! I was screwed from the beginning!

Now that the courtyard was mine once again, I closed my eyes and spent some time on a solo review meeting.

Once the Max can in my hand had grown somewhat lukewarm, untouched by my lips, I heard the crunching sound of footsteps on gravel.

"Heeey, you!" a sweet voice called out to me lightly, and I turned toward it.

For an instant, a soft, chilly sensation touched my cheek. When I bent back in surprise, Iroha Isshiki, who I'd thought had passed by just a moment ago, was standing right there, grinning mischievously with an I LOHAS bottled water in her hand. *Aha, so then she's a booth babe handing out freebies? She's just that cute. What the heck, too cute.*

"H-hey... What, is something up?" I asked, rattled. The unspoken question was: *Didn't you go back to class?*

Isshiki plopped herself down on the bench and said nonchalantly, "I said I was stopping by the student council room and slipped out."

"Uh-huh..."

Despite her claim, she showed no sign of heading to the student council room. Instead, she touched the plastic bottle in her hand to her forehead, then blew out an exhausted-sounding sigh. "When you say you're going to the washroom or to go buy a drink or something, everyone just follows you, you know?" she said as she shook the plastic bottle in her hands. Ah, so this I LOHAS had been bought as an excuse to get away from her friends.

"Huh. Well, the new semester can be like that. You wind up going together for everything."

Isshiki nodded back at me and inched one fist's worth closer. "For suuure. That's why it's a good thing I can bring up the student council...y'know, for times like these."

"True, it's a handy excuse. I get that, I get that." At this school, only Iroha Isshiki had the character class of student council president. So she only had to bring that up whenever she wanted to relax on her own. *I see, very convenient.*

When I nodded along, Isshiki stared dully back at me. "Do you really get it?"

"Yeah. It's just like when you're coming back from a meeting outside of work or school, and you're going in the same direction as someone you've only just met, and it's just so awkward that you start lying like, *Oh, I have something to do after this...* to shake them off."

"Agh, that's totally different..." Isshiki sighed weakly and with utter exasperation. Then she lightly touched a hand to her chest and leaned in slightly to peer at my face. "That's not what I mean..." She trailed off there, and then as if imparting a secret, she brought her lips close to my ear and whispered softly, "...I mean times like *this.*"

No one was even here, but the way she lowered her lovely voice felt like a brief play bite on my earlobes.

"Uh...yeah, for sure. Times like this, huh? Right, so anyway, what—what's up? What did you want?" I leaned away to escape the floral scent and the ticklishness, grasping for words to cover my embarrassment.

Isshiki nimbly came away. "Nothing in particular... Wait, you were the one looking at me. I thought that meant you wanted me to come over here. I mean, when I waved, you ignored it."

"No way could I respond to you then... I don't want to act weird; then my friends would spread rumors about me..."

My charmingly bashful ploy, worthy of the heroines of old classic games, did little to affect Isshiki's expression. "What?"

Hmm, maybe she's too young for that one. She looked really, actually serious, not even prepping some comeback like *You don't have any friends, though.*

I remember having an exchange like this before, I thought, letting out a tiny nostalgic chuckle through my nose.

Meanwhile, Isshiki was sighing again. "Well, some boys are like that, huh. They won't talk to you unless they have a reason. Which also means they'll make up some stupid reason to pester you with an attempt at conversation."

"Hey, stop it—some guys can do their best if they have a chance. Stop it."

But Isshiki wasn't listening. "Here I am thinking, *You don't have to bother coming all the way to me to ask what'll be on the test; you should just ask your friends over there*, and then they try to keep it going on forever on LINE and you pretend to fall asleep, y'knooow?"

"Stop it, stop it, stop it. Stop prodding the soft spots of middle school boys. Especially me. Sometimes one small action can change the world… I do believe that…"

Everything is like that. With a twist on the everyday, you can change the world. Let me change the world… I want to make miracles with you…

As I was gazing far off into the distance while mentally assembling my prayer of complaint, Isshiki watched me with a veeery dull look in her eyes, but that eventually turned into a smile that silently asked, *What can you do?* "Do you do that in your classroom, too? I know we just got new classes."

"Well, yeah. And once you're in third year, you'll be somewhat familiar with basically everyone, so people aren't really trying to go out and build new relationships—and I don't just mean with me. So there isn't really a need to talk with anyone."

That was ultimately nothing more than my impression as an

outsider, but Isshiki gave my views an *mm-hmm*. "I see... Well, you already are in third year, huh?"

"Yeah, I'm in third year...," I said, before my voice darkened a little. "So now I've got different problems."

Isshiki cocked her head, which made her pale hair swish down to hang over her white throat. Pushing aside the hairs that caught on her colored lip gloss, Isshiki wordlessly asked for me to continue.

I quickly folded my arms and let my tone darken a little more as I went on. "Some kids will start calling anything *the last one of high school*, and it gets a little obnoxious..."

The troublesome thing about remarks like these is the fact that they aren't entirely wrong. You could even say this moment right now would be my own last something of high school.

It's not like I don't understand the desire to describe everything as "the last X of high school," but if you say that, then every single day winds up commemorating something. So you're Machi Tawara, huh?

It seemed my weariness had come out pretty clearly, regardless of my intentions. Isshiki made a face, too. "Ahhh, like a couple who've just started dating having an anniversary of whatever..."

"Yeah, yeah."

"Yeah, that is a little annoying... When they post that stuff on social media, you're like, *Ugh shut up, who cares*, and you have to hit Like anyway."

"Y-yeah, yeah..." I thought I'd been doing well listening along, but then suddenly, I stuttered. *I see—so Irohasu is the type who will make sure to press Like, even if she secretly hates it. How nice...* I have absolutely no plans to post anything about anniversaries on social media, but that got me thinking that I should try to avoid making people feel bad.

But even I am merely human. It's not like I don't get wanting to make an anniversary special.

Everyone will have one or two dates they'd like to remember. Even a trivial day of little importance can be an irreplaceable anniversary to someone.

The biggest example of this is birthdays.

Thinking of that, I picked up the Max can I'd left on the bench beside me and held it out to Isshiki. "Want this?"

"What? Uh, randomly offering someone a half-drunk drink is actually a crime, though." Isshiki scoot-scoot-scooted over to the edge of the bench, raising up both hands in front of her chest in a total defensive stance.

"I haven't even had any yet... Look. This tab is totally untouched. Pretty, isn't it? This is unopened, you know?" To prove that, I waved the can and emphasized my innocence.

That seemed to win her over, as she inched back closer to her original position. Then she reached out with trepidation to accept the canned coffee from me. "Agh, well, thanks... Might as well take it, then. I'm not really sure if I'll drink it, though..."

She is brutally honest, huh...? But I think it's nice, the way she won't flatly reject another's goodwill, even when she's reluctant.

"Happy birthday," I said with a wry smile, putting the drink in her hand.

But there was no answer from her. She stared dumbly at the Max can enveloped in her hands.

"..." She blinked, expression vacant, and then all I heard was an unvoiced breath.

When I asked her with a look, *What is it?* she snapped out of it with a gasp and started fidgeting with her bangs. "...Y-you remembered, huh? You didn't say anything, so I thought for sure you'd forgotten."

"Nah, there just wasn't the right moment to say it..." When I'd first caught sight of Isshiki, she'd been too far away, and once we'd started talking, that surprise bottled water attack had made it out of the question for the moment...

But I couldn't possibly forget Iroha Isshiki's birthday. She'd taken every opportunity to draw attention to it before, and most of all, for these past few days, the subject had been the talk of the Service Club, of which I was a member. Apparently, that day after school, the whole club was going to throw a surprise party.

But even if we were arranging a surprise, it would be too suspicious not to mention anything birthday adjacent even when I ran into her. When you get to a sensitivity championship of my level, you'll see right through that stuff and think, *That's odd... It's my birthday today, but nobody's saying happy birthday to me... Aha! So they're planning a surprise?* And then the day just ends with nothing happening. That's happened to me before.

If I anticipated such thoughts and wished Isshiki happy birthday now, I would be able to divert her attention away from hopes for or suspicion of a surprise. The plan here was to double the effect of the surprise. An absolutely enchanting play, if I do say so myself...

As I was feeling smug, there was a tugging on my sleeve. When I looked over like, *What's up?* I saw Isshiki was turned away, pouting.

"One can of coffee isn't enough, you know," she muttered sulkily. "I'm not that cheap."

I know. I do have my own sort of present for you... So I wanted to say, but I swallowed it. I had to leave that for the surprise after school.

Despite her insistence about her worth, Isshiki didn't throw the Max can back at me and just tucked it into her blazer pocket.

Instead, she offered me something else. "...Um, here, I'll give you this."

"Oh, thanks." I reflexively gave a *Thank you, I accept...* sort of bow as I took the I LOHAS she had been holding.

"...Huh? What?" I glanced up from my hands at Isshiki.

She was still looking away, but she answered my question surprisingly directly. "It's a trade...for the coffee."

I see. I don't get it. Why did this girl give me an I LOHAS? I could explain the Max can as a birthday gift. But I couldn't think of any reason for me to get something from her.

"Oh-ho..." *So then is this the straw millionaire thing?* I wondered, staring in confusion at the flavored water in my hands.

Isshiki cleared her throat with a loud *hmmm!* Then she jabbed a finger at me and puffed up her cheeks in a pout, as if to cover their redness. "…It's an exchange, okay?! So the present you just gave me is null and void!"

"Huh…?" *Is that how presents work? Are you even if you give something back?*

Isshiki ignored my confusion and briskly moved the conversation along. "Sooo you can give me a present later… How about this weekend? I'm free, you know?"

"Huh? Ah, um, I was more or less considering getting you something else…" *I even planned to give it to you after school…* So I wanted to say, but since there was a surprise party, I couldn't tell her straight. Oh, dilemma!

However Isshiki took my silence, she smiled brightly and leaned forward on the bench. She gently laid one hand on my shoulder and cupped the other around her mouth. And then with a sweet, syrupy suggestion in her tone, Iroha Isshiki brought her lips close and whispered, "The present is an excuse."

Before I could ask what for in a totally transparent attempt to play dumb, Isshiki popped away again and smiled as if nothing had happened.

My sigh was drowned out by the bell alerting us to the start of class, and Isshiki stood up at the same moment and continued to walk a few steps away. And then with a light flutter of her skirt, she turned back again.

As if to say she wouldn't even bother listening to my reply, she waved and said, "Then I'm looking forward to the weekend!" before hurrying off to the school building.

"O-okay…" There was nothing for it but to reply with a bewildered nod at her retreating back, even knowing she wouldn't see it.

By force of gradual erosion, my weekend plans had been decided.

Oh, I'd expect nothing less of Irohasu.

The way she 100 percent recycled the plastic bottle she'd just bought and then connected it to a future activity was awe-inspiring. *She doesn't just have me in the palm of her hand—she's got me wrapped all the way around her little finger, too...*

I didn't know how many more times we would repeat that same old exchange. I could swear her tactics were the same as ever, and yet they somehow felt like they had evolved—to become even more cunningly, cutely clever.

A casual and nonchalant accumulation of mundane experiences. That single action had clearly moved my heart and was assembling the future ahead of us.

Irohasu really is the greatest...

But surely, **the girls** will also continue to go wrong.

The spring was coming to an end, and the scent of early summer was beginning to waft in the air.

In the courtyard below the aerial walkway, new green budded at the ends of the tree branches, which were softly swaying in the refreshing breeze. All the white flower petals had left the cherry trees, but the green was still too slight to say the trees were in leaf. Once that green grew a little denser, the "new school year" mood would settle down.

Around this time of year, clear lines were drawn between those who had managed to build relationships due to an inherent ability to get along, those who had managed to turn over a new leaf and start a better life in high school, and those who hadn't managed to fit in well and chose to commit to noble lonerdom.

Though you can't generalize to say which side of this deal is the better one.

Even if you do have someone to talk to or someone to pair up with in gym class, that's not necessarily fortunate. Building a relationship with someone also often means touching the fetters of obligation that person bears.

Friendships are not made up of a single friend unit. Whether you like it or not, you're also forced into second-degree contact with their relationships—such as a friend of a friend, or a friend's girlfriend, or someone your friend hates.

You can't be mean to people your friends are close to; if your friend has a girlfriend, you'll show at least some consideration for her; and it's also difficult to be friends with someone your own friend hates. Those who know this discomfort might say being alone is preferable.

And yet I was currently immobilized by such fetters in my new class.

Since seat numbers are assigned based on syllabic order, in most classes aside from electives, I almost always get stuck next to Hayato Hayama. It's a lot of trouble to manage. As for what that trouble is— it's the fact that Ebina often talks with Hayama, which brings her near me.

Nobody is harder to deal with than someone you're only somewhat acquainted with.

Well, I have gotten somewhat used to Hayama, so it's not so bad with him.

We both just selfishly talk at each other, with no expectation of establishing any proper communication. Since neither of us really listens to what the other says, any sudden silences aren't really uncomfortable.

Ultimately, we just assume we each understand what the other is really thinking and monologue back and forth, so conversation and silence mean basically the same thing.

If you think about it that way, then my conversations with Hayama are less to worry about.

…But in those odd moments when I wind up alone with Ebina, I really don't know what to do.

I have no idea what topics might be sensitive for her, so when she suddenly falls silent, I wonder if I said something wrong. Times like that, I always find myself thinking, *Hayama! Hurry and get over here!*

Well, from my experience with Hayama and Ebina in second year, I've somewhat managed to figure out how to interact with them.

The problem is people other than Hayama.

It goes without saying at this point, but Hayama will always attract attention. Not only during breaks, but in classes like gym and stuff where there tends to be downtime, people often approach him to chat. My adjacent seat number often results in me getting incorporated into that circle.

Maybe they were enthusiastic about making new friends because it was a new semester, or maybe it was because all our classmates were friendly people, but whenever I was going hard into silent Jizo statue mode, they tried to be considerate and involve me in the conversation when they were chatting with Hayama. Like an afterthought.

Frankly, it can be brutal making conversation just for the sake of filling out awkward moments with people whose names I couldn't quite place—but even I am merely human. I would feel bad to disregard the kindness of others.

And so, every time they tried to involve me, I'd generally just find the right moments to place a "Yeah, I dunno," "Not like I know," "Whoa," "It's hard to explain," "For sure" on the metaphorical conveyor belt of conversation, somehow getting through it by milking the sort of conversational skills anyone can manage.

When you do this, just about everyone will give you an awkward look: *This really isn't going anywhere...* You can't even get a discussion going. It's like their communication skills are massively underdeveloped. If I can manage to talk with these socially awkward people, then I can finally call myself a skilled communicator, huh? And, like, maybe I'll be able to manage by the time I have to get a job?

Anyway, this sort of rhythm-game-esque garbage conversation often generates a silence. And it's Hayama and Ebina who fill up that space.

Thanks to them, I've come to be known as "the guy Hayama and Ebina are babysitting."

Considering I'd gotten the absolute worst pull in the class gacha (where you can't reinstall and try again), I could call this a surprisingly smooth start. The bar is real low, huh...?

Once you reach your third year of high school, you don't expect much from relationships with your classmates.

I figured the world never really changes; so long as time went by with no major mishaps, I was fine with that—a sort of pseudo-enlightened resignation. But this is ultimately the view of someone who has grown world-weary, worn, and frayed at the edges.

Then what about the new boys and girls at our school? I thought, suddenly curious about how my own little sister, Komachi Hikigaya, was faring in her new life.

She had entered Soubu High School that spring to officially become my junior, but I couldn't possibly know the whole picture of her time at school. Of course, I did see her at our club, and we did have a variety of talks about things at home, but I didn't know how she was doing in her class.

She had eagerly put on her uniform for a solo fashion show during spring break, and once school started, she'd been humming cheerily as she made her commute with me. But lately, I'd gotten the impression her giddiness had settled quite a bit.

No matter what sort of new life you start, with each passing day, its vividness will turn into something more peaceful.

Especially with high school, when you're cooped up in one room seeing the same faces of your classmates every day, you come to remember their names at least vaguely, and you get a grasp of their modes of life based on the bits of conversations they have or the kinds of things they do during breaks.

Once a month or so has passed, you get the gist of their superficial personalities and the positions they occupy in the class, and relationships in general start to firm up.

I wasn't that worried about Komachi, given how good she is with people, but still, worrying is just what a big brother does.

All righty then, however is Komachi doing at school? I wondered as I headed off to the Service Club.

My fingers touched the clubroom door, and when I opened it with

a rattle, there was Komachi, resting her chin on her hand and absent-mindedly gazing out the window.

She must have been studying for the midterm that was looming in two weeks, or perhaps she was simply killing time; her textbook and notebook were spread open on her desk, but her mechanical pencil was not in her hand, instead lying forlornly atop her notebook.

At the sound of the door, Komachi's listless expression turned into a bright smile. "Ohhh, Bro."

"Hey, you're early," I said as I headed for the seat that, at some point, had become my spot.

"Well, if Komachi doesn't come, it won't get unlocked." She shrugged casually with a little chuckle before picking up the mechanical pencil, flipping through her notebook, and resuming her studying.

It had been just about a month since the Service Club had been remade.

Along with the seat of club captain, Komachi had also taken on the job of locking and unlocking the clubroom door, and it was fair to say she'd been doing a satisfactory job. Since she was coming first to the clubroom every single time, she really was handling it well.

Thinking about it now, the former captain had also come to the clubroom before anyone else, and it seemed that strict conscientiousness had been passed on to the next generation.

Then thinking about Yukinoshita made me remember. "Yukinoshita and Yuigahama said they're not coming today," I said.

"Yeah, I heard," Komachi answered without looking up from her textbook.

"Oh, okay…"

Well, she was basically the club captain, so she would be keeping in contact with the relevant parties. Komachi didn't ask the reason for their absence and instead just skritched along with her mechanical pencil.

Well, not that I want her to ask why.

This was part of the surprise.

It had been about one month since Komachi had assumed the office of Service Club captain. These days, we were just getting used to this new organizational structure. Yukinoshita and Yuigahama had come up with the idea of giving her a present to celebrate becoming club captain, and then we decided to make it a surprise.

I did briefly think, *If it's just a present for a party or anniversary, then just give it to her normally...* But presenting it on an ordinary day would actually make it more of a surprise.

I tend to find myself wondering what might happen around every single turning point, not only birthdays. An old man going to work on his last day before retirement totally expects to get a bouquet, after all. So from this perspective, even Komachi wasn't going to assume she would get a present around now. This wasn't even a one-month anniversary.

To leverage this surprise to the utmost, it was vital to keep Komachi from being suspicious. If all three of us were out at once, she'd obviously wonder if something was up. I was here to create an alibi, to keep her from getting suspicious.

So it was a welcome thing to be spared the extra work. I doubt I could really fool Komachi entirely. Maybe Yukinoshita and Yuigahama had taken that into consideration, and that was why they'd contacted her.

Long story short, Yukinoshita and Yuigahama were both busy, so Komachi and I would be all alone for club time that day.

The sound of her mechanical pencil was particularly loud in the silent clubroom.

Even though we were often alone together at home, and it was common for us to spend time not really talking and just petting the cat, this quiet bothered me a lot. Was it because we hadn't really ever been alone together in the clubroom specifically before? I just felt weirdly anxious.

But I'm too shy to just say that... So I found myself laying out my books on my desk, even though I normally never do.

Might as well follow Komachi's lead and study. I clicked at the head of my mechanical pencil and started scribbling out the answers to the set of problems in my notebook.

It tended to slip my mind—or rather I wanted it to—but despite appearances, I was a student in preparation for university entrance exams. I had to take these spare moments here and there to study.

Our mechanical pencils made light sounds for a while, playing a mild ensemble.

We never even studied together at home, so I couldn't keep my attention from sliding to the presence sitting diagonally across from me. Tap-tapping the end of my mechanical pencil on my notebook, I pretended to think while I glanced over to check on her.

A month had passed since she'd started at this school, so I was used to seeing her in the uniform: blazer with slightly overlong sleeves, blouse with the first collar button open, a loosely tied ribbon. It was normal enough to me that I could really examine her.

Hmm…

Now that I'm seeing her properly, she looks pretty good in that. If I may say so of my own sister, she is hyper-cute at the very least.

While she still had a girlish innocence, the playful hairpin that clipped her bangs and her casually worn uniform had a liveliness in them. She gave off a sense of carefree cheer.

I was sure she was popular in her class. In the "Cutest Girl in Our Class Derby" that the boys would be doubtless be holding regularly, they'd probably be having conversations like *The most popular is, of course, this one, Komachi Hikigaya!* and *She's the classmate I'm most looking forward to seeing more of! I hope she gives it all she's got!* and then she'd be the favorite to win the race. What? Hey, you're looking at my little sister in *that* way? I'll kill you? (dark smile)

Knowing nothing of what was going through my head, Komachi just read through her textbook, making the cowlick sticking up on top of her head boing back and forth with each thoughtful nod.

She tucked the hairs that swished down behind her ear, then stuck her red pen back there, too, while her highlighter squeaked across the paper. Then she smooshed the marker against her cheek and cocked her head, apparently checking her work.

She must have sensed my gaze then, as she glanced over at me. Then with a mildly disgruntled look, she opened her mouth. "What?"

"Nothing," I said, shaking my head ever so slightly. *No, really, it's nothing.* I did want to say *Close your blouse button*, but if I carp at her about that, she'll hate me…

Komachi huffed out her nose in dissatisfaction, and then she dropped her eyes to her textbook once more.

The conversation ended there, replaced by the squeak of her high-lighter, the skritching of her red pen drawing circles, and then some bored groaning from me.

Now that I was actually watching Komachi study in uniform, I really couldn't help but worry about how she was doing. Is my dear girl like this in her classes, too, I wonder?

Once I was struck with the urge to visit her class, a fatherly mood rose inside me. I cleared my throat and opened a reference book with a rustle of pages. "…How's school?"

Despite creating a weighty atmosphere of importance, the words came out too curt. You couldn't even tell who I was muttering at, and our eyes didn't meet, either.

That line and that gesture were the image of the mid-century dad at the breakfast table, first spreading out a newspaper to speak to his adolescent son… Those dads are way too socially awkward, aren't they?

Komachi could only stare back at me. Then she cracked an exasperated smile. "Who's that supposed to be? Dad? And we're at the same school."

"Oh, well, I mean, we do see each other in the clubroom, but I don't know how things are in your class." I was a little unhappy about being put in the same category as our father, but I had been just about to ask slightly more intrusive things, like *Have you made friends?* or *Think you can get a boyfriend?* Can't blame her for calling me Dad!

Whenever my parents asked me questions like that, I always wished earnestly for them to leave me alone, so I'd like to give myself credit for not picking those ones.

My feelings must have gotten across, because Komachi folded her arms with a *hmm* as she tried to give me a real answer. "Hmm... Well, true." Tilting her head, she groaned again, but eventually, her head popped up again, and she replied with a super-serious expression, "Normal."

"I see..." Well, that was the only answer to give. I would answer the same if our parents asked that, too.

It's too much of a hassle to explain any friendships in detail, especially school friends. I don't want to make them worry, but also, talking about stuff like that directly with them is embarrassing.

So that limits you to the use of three remarks: "Okay," "Nothing much," and "Normal."

Yeah, yeah. I get that, I get that.

But I was still worried anyway, so I couldn't not ask. I've recently come to learn how a parent feels, wavering between helicoptering and nonintervention.

When Komachi was little, she'd come to me to report all sorts of things. Listen, listen! *she'd say, or* Hey, so Komachi did... *But then she's grown up so fast. She's fully in puberty now,* I thought, a single tear forming in my eye.

But Komachi waved her hands, expression serious. "No, no, not a rebellious phase. It really is just normal. Komachi does have friends like normal, and I'm keeping up with my classes like normal, and I'm enjoying myself like normal. So, well, normal?" she said. Her expression was very flat—indeed normal. From her face and the way she talked, I didn't get the sense that she was trying to cover or avoid anything.

She had to be having a peaceful time at school, without any major complaints, grievances, or anxieties. Maybe it was so peaceful, she had to use the world *normal* to explain it. If that's what she was going to say, then I had no choice but to accept it.

"Oh, I see... All right, then," I said.

Komachi nodded. "Yeah. Or, like, you're the only one who's in a rebellious phase, Bro. Komachi normally talks about school with Mom, too."

"Huhhh...... What about Dad?" I asked.

"Eh-heh-heh. Dad's busy, so..." Komachi laughed cutely, avoiding the question.

But that wasn't necessarily a complete lie. Our father was actually busy at work every day, so it was true enough there wasn't much overlap in our lifestyle time slots. On weekends, Dad and I would both be sleeping hard, so we ultimately only saw each other around mealtimes. Well, Mom's also busy, too. Since both our parents have the inheritance factors "Corporate slave ☆☆☆," at this rate, I'll wind up inheriting that, too.

As I was trembling with such thoughts, Komachi cleared her throat and stabbed a finger at me. "And hey, you don't talk with Dad, either."

"That's not true. I'm always talking with him about how he should give me money," I said proudly.

"Whaa...? That's even meaner than Komachi..." She drew away in horror.

But I can't help that—I'm too busy studying for entrance exams, so I can't get a part-time job. Being in this position is costly in various ways, what with buying reference books and taking mock tests and such. Making the fullest use of this to come up with suitable reasons to extort money from him is my main source of income.

"But that's the only common topic of conversation I have with Dad. There's nothing for it, right?"

"That's a sad father-son relationship... Your own flesh and blood can't come up with a topic of conversation...," Komachi muttered sorrowfully as she gave me a pitying look.

"Well, that's just how it is with fathers and sons, not like I know. All you can talk about is money, or your impressions of the new *Evangelion*."

"Hmm... You've got a closer father-son relationship than Komachi thought..." Komachi's expression shifted from its former sorrow to a mildly discomfited wry smile. She was even pulling away slightly.

Well, it's no wonder she would be put off by that... My dad and I are both the same in that once we start talking about our opinions, all we can say is "Thanks..." It hardly ever turns into a real conversation... Most people would get weirded out seeing us—two guys hardly meeting each other's eyes, looking into blank space as they say "Thanks..."

Well, Dad's one thing, but if Komachi was talking about school with our mom, then she should be fine.

She said so herself; she was having a normal, good, uneventful, and unchanging time at school.

"...Well, so long as you're not having any particular problems, okay then," I said.

"Mm-hmm." And then Komachi nodded back at me and faced her textbook again.

I watched her until my mind started to drift.

A pleasant wind was blowing through the open window.

In the distance, I could hear the vigorous calls of sports club members cheering for their teammates, as well as out-of-tune notes from the brass band.

It sounded like there were new members in all the clubs. The after-school melody had become more irregular, but that just gave it an extra shot of lively energy.

Right now it was all disharmony, but with each following day, they would fall into sync, and eventually, it would become beautiful background music that we would remember fondly.

Inclining my ears to the sounds out the window, I turned my head to survey the clubroom.

The room was quiet, with just the scratching of a mechanical pencil and the occasional slide of a turning page.

The feeling that came over me was something like nostalgia—had the room been this big before? My eyes lay still on Komachi, who was sitting diagonally across from me.

The two of us were alone.

Komachi was silently reading her textbook, seemingly undistracted by anything.

The image was similar to the scene I'd witnessed in this clubroom just one year ago.

A girl reading a book in the slanting light.

It was a vivid reminder of her, back then.

If I hadn't been dragged here on that day, would she still be reading alone here in this room, unchanging?

What a pointless thing to imagine.

No matter how you wonder about what-ifs, you can't turn back time. Even if I could do it over, if I couldn't carry forward this memory, the result still wouldn't change. In the end, I would have been brought to this room.

So there was no point in this line of thought.

But if I were to try to find a point...

...I could say this hypothetical was a hint to how Komachi might be someday.

I would only be able to stay in this clubroom a bit longer. Graduation was waiting in less than a year. After we'd left, would she still be here, passing the mundane hours after school by herself? Here in this room, without the girls and no scent of tea?

The idea made my heart clench.

I'd known it would happen eventually, but it hadn't felt real until I saw Komachi alone in the clubroom like this.

"Komachi," I said. Her face popped up, and she tilted her head to ask without words, *What?*

"Do you wanna recruit new members?" I said with no preface at all.

She blinked. Eventually, surprise and confusion showed on her face. "Where's this coming from...?"

"I mean, the other clubs have new members... I was thinking it'd be nice if we had some younger members, too." I couldn't say that it was because I'd just imagined a scenario that had prickled my heart, so I chose to be evasive instead.

Komachi narrowed her eyes at me. "Bro, I thought stuff like that was too much trouble for you. Like, you treat Taishi so bad."

"That's not true. I don't hate hierarchical relationships when I'm the one on top." I puffed out my chest.

Komachi was horrified. "The worst kind of senior…"

"Anyway, Taishi's…you know. Not really a junior, more like Kawa-something's little brother, or Keika's older brother." Taishi would indeed count as my junior at school, but since I've known him from before he came to this school, I didn't really think of him that way.

If we became members of the same club or something and saw each other on a daily basis, I'm sure that relationship value would be updated, and I would be able to recognize him as my junior, but at this point, he was stuck as a maggot who had come near Komachi.

…*Of course if I say anything about maggots or whatnot, Komachi will get upset with me again. Let's not share that one*, I thought, swallowing my words.

Komachi continued to look at me skeptically; she could probably tell I was trying not to say something unkind.

But upon hearing the pleasant sound of a metal bat and an off-key trumpet, she slid her gaze out the window. "To be honest, Komachi's also thought about…" She gave a weak sigh.

Apparently, I didn't even have to worry about it, because Komachi was thinking about the future, too. *Phew…*

But that relief only lasted a brief moment, as Komachi folded her arms with a *hmm*, making a face that put a wrinkle between her eyes. "Even if we were gonna recruit people, it's hard to explain this club, you know."

"Ahhh…yeah." That got an automatic agreement from me. This club probably did seem pretty inscrutable to other people.

Despite being called the Service Club, it wasn't like we were engaged in any service activity or what you might call "volunteer activities." Lately, we had functionally become subcontractors for the student council, and the consultation and requests that occasionally came in were all very personal matters. It would be hard to explain to a third party.

It's different if you have a straightforward goal like with baseball, soccer, or rugby, such as Koshien, nationals, or Hanazono, but unfortunately, I've never heard of anything like an "Advice Consultation World Championship."

I remembered before, when we were preparing for the Christmas event and I'd run into Kaori Orimoto, she'd burst out laughing, and I repeated what she'd told me then. "If you say 'We're the Service Club,' it's just like… 'What does that club do?'"

"Hmm… Yeah, our activities are one thing, but there's a lot of other things, too…," Komachi said with a wry smile, then nodded and took us back to the beginning of this talk. "Well, what we do is kind of annoying and kinda unique, so I think it might be okay not to push canvassing. When you don't fit in, you just quit, right? Like you with your part-time jobs," she said, sticking up her index finger and wagging it.

"Y-yeah… Well, that's true…" Using me as an example was a convincing argument. Once you get to be a golden flaker-outer of my level, you just need to make one application phone call to pick up on the atmosphere of the workplace and then flake out of the interview.

Plus, people flaking out is rampant even with part-time jobs you can get paid for, so with a club where you work for free, I wouldn't be surprised if they dropped out in seconds.

We could work our butts off canvassing, but if they just quit anyway, we'd wind up right back where we started. In fact, we'd even be out the cost of advertising.

We couldn't just aimlessly canvass. We also had to put in some effort to keep people from quitting.

I hear these days, all the corporate slaves are working hard to keep new employees from quitting… And when they train the new employees, they get directions from HR saying not to upset the newbies. But really, shouldn't reevaluating the system of employment and wages come first? If they worked four days a week for a generous ten-million-yen salary, they'd never quit, you know?

But it wasn't the time for me to be thinking about my future. This was about the future of the Service Club.

It was too uncertain whether a total outsider would be able to fit in with this incomprehensible club. It would be faster to go scout someone who'd fit in from the start, best we could tell. This is what you'd call head-hunting.

"What about your friends?" I asked her. "Nobody wanting to offer some service?"

"Huhhh…? That sounds like you're looking for a maid… And it's not like Komachi wants to do any service work…" She twisted up her lips like *eugh*.

What a coincidence, I don't have even a sliver of service spirit, either. If neither the club captain nor the members have any interest in service, then…what does this club do?

As I momentarily pondered this, Komachi put a hand to her jaw. "Hmm, well, I think my friends probably won't want to. They're either already in clubs, or they've decided they weren't going to join any."

"Huhhh… Yeah, by this time, I guess they would already be in one," I said.

Komachi shrugged with a wry smile. "Basically."

It had been about one month since the start of the year.

The period for trying out clubs would soon be over, and those first-years with the motivation would be focusing their efforts in the clubs they had aspirations for.

But nobody had shown up to join as a temporary member or sit in on the Service Club, which brought us to the present.

Part of why we hadn't done anything to secure new members was that we'd all been busy since the joint prom, so I was forced to admit there was nothing we could do. We hadn't even expected the Service Club would keep going in the first place, so we hadn't made any preparations.

I racked my brain. *Should we start doing something now, mayhap…?*

But Komachi was the one at the center of this, and she didn't seem to care. "Well, there's no point in rushing it. It'll be okay for a while like this. Komachi'll think about members later."

"Yeah?" I said with full skepticism.

Komachi nodded. "Yeah... Besides, it's not so bad for Komachi to get this room to herself." A nasty smirk rose on her face.

"Ohhh... Like, hearing you put it that way, now I'm kinda jealous..."

"Right, right? It's like my own private room at school. I'm a VIP." She chuckled smugly, with silly gestures as if she was about to break into a cheery little dance.

But my brain couldn't help but pull up that scene I'd imagined before, and I found a touch of sadness in that smile.

I didn't know what Komachi was really thinking behind those words.

But she was the one who had rebooted the Service Club, and she was in charge. I would be leaving in less than a year, so maybe it wasn't something I should be cutting in on.

Just... if it's possible...

I was unconsciously looking at the door.

If possible, if someone would appear like on that day without knocking, flinging open that rattly door...

It was a terribly selfish desire.

But then suddenly, that door shuddered and clunked. Komachi noticed it, too, and looked over as it slowly opened.

A warm but refreshing summer breeze blew from the window into the hallway. The wind swished through the visitor's pale hair and ribbon at her chest.

Without asking permission, she marched into the room like she owned the place—Iroha Isshiki.

"Heeeey, guys." Closing the rattling and creaking door behind her, she stuck up two fingers in a *yo* sort of wave.

When Komachi saw her, a smile appeared as if she was too exhausted to stop it.

× × ×

Iroha Isshiki was both the student council president and the soccer club manager.

And, if I may add, not a member of the Service Club.

And yet you just keep showing up here... Eh, it's totally okay, though. So long as you don't bring any land mines that are gonna be a huge hassle.

Well, well, whatever is my lady's business this fine morrow? I looked over at Isshiki to see her taking a seat in the chair that had been designated hers at some point. She was glancing all around the room.

"...Ummm, sooo where are Yukino and Yui? They not here today?" Isshiki's gaze drifted to the two empty seats. Normally, that was where Yukinoshita and Yuigahama would be sitting, but unfortunately, they were off that day.

"They said they had some stuff to do, so they're not coming," I answered.

"Yep, yep, so today is Komachi and Bro working as a pair," Komachi added.

Isshiki put a hand to her chin. "*Mgh.* Really? Oh, darn..."

"Huh, what...? Is there some kind of problem?" I asked, fearing she might have come here with another unreasonable demand from the student council.

Isshiki beamed a bright smile and then nonchalantly remarked: "No, just thinking the tea server isn't here..."

"Just what do you take Yukinoshita for?" I said with a scandalized look. *She better not think the Service Club is a café or something...*

Isshiki clunked her forehead with a *tee-hee-blep-bonk*, shooting off a wink and sticking out her tongue with a smile. "Just kidding. ♪"

I would no longer be fooled by that; it was way past the point now where I would think, *Aw nooo, this girl is soo cunning-cute!* But she is cute... She *is* cute, but that's that and this is this, and I had to ask the nature of her business. I mean, she is cute, though?

"Oh, then Komachi will pour the tea today," Komachi said.

"Thanks, Okome-chaaaan! ☆" Isshiki tittered *tee-hee*.

Komachi replied "It's nothing, it's nothing" as she rose from her seat.

Wow, that Okome-chan nickname has actually stuck... Maybe I'll call her Rice-chan at home, too! But Rice-chan won't call me "Brother" in that refined and respectful way, I mused as Rice-chan skillfully prepared the tea.

But I couldn't just sit around like this, waiting for the tea to be served. I glanced over at Isshiki, prompting her to continue like, *So, what're you here for?* She'd just muttered "Oh darn," so it was probably some new hassle.

When Isshiki saw me look at her, she cleared her throat. "If you *muuust* call it work, then yes, I did more or less come with work. There was a little something I wanted to ask you about..." She put her index finger to the end of her chin, cocked her head, and sighed. I could tell she was worrying about whether to bring it up.

Then her gaze moved to the empty seats.

Hmm, I don't know what she came to ask us about, but it seems like she wanted Yukinoshita and Yuigahama to hear it. Nothing for it but to get her to come back another day...

But before I could say anything, Komachi jumped on it. "Oooh, a request?" Her eyes sparkled, filled with eagerness.

Well, the Service Club was for getting requests and consultations and stuff. Maybe she was excited to finally get some activity that was Service Club–like.

Komachi quickly finished preparing the tea, switched the electric kettle on, and bounced back to her original seat.

Then she turned to Isshiki and swished the hair off her shoulders with the back of her hand.

Uh, your hair isn't long enough to swish..., I thought, and then Komachi swished it back a second and third time with an incredibly serene smile on her face. "Then let's hear what you have to say. Please take a seat," she said, putting on an extremely composed persona as she indicated Isshiki's seat.

This left Isshiki bewildered, mouth half-open. "No, no, I'm already sitting... Wait, is that your Yukino impression? Ha-ha! It's nothing like her... Wait, actually, it kinda is like her."

Komachi swished her hair back again as if batting away Isshiki's half laugh, then touched that hand to her lips. "Komachi is simply conducting herself as the club president. Komachi wouldn't designate this as an impression of Yukino." Komachi's impression of Yukino Yukinoshita was getting more and more exaggerated.

"Ohhh, you nailed it—she does talk pretentiously like that." Isshiki jabbed a finger at her like, *That's it!* and burst into giggles.

C'mon now, girls. Don't, like, be a jerk or whatever.

I considered telling them off in a *gyaru*-like way, but making jokes at the expense of people higher than you on the food chain, mainly when they're not in the room, is just what younger people do. It would be crass to stop such behavior. I dunno why I needed to be a *gyaru*, either.

But don't take it too far, now... If she saw that impression, she'd get very huffy about it. Well, her sulky mood has its own appeal..., I thought as the two girls further entertained themselves with impressions of their elders.

"Huhhh. So then maybe I'll try practicing *yahallo*," said Isshiki.

"Ohhh! I'd love to see you go all in on a yahallo!" Komachi replied. "That would be hilarious all by itself."

"...Hold up? *Hilarious* is kind of a weird word to use. You don't mean it like laughing *at* me, do you?"

"No, no, not *pffft* at all."

"You're totally laughing at me..."

Despite this conversation, I doubt Yuigahama would be mad if Isshiki did greet people with *yahallo*.

However, that would be forgiven precisely because Yuigahama and Isshiki had a trusting relationship. If someone not all that close to her—like Zaimokuza or the UG club guys, for example—teased her about it, that would honestly be really scary. She'd be like, *Stop it* in a low tone of voice, and then it'd be like, *Oh shit, she's actually mad. ...Though I* suppose that's also nice for what it is. Like how she'll occasionally let her genuine anger show—I can kinda get into that? This Hachiman guy is always getting into everything.

But anyway, teasing someone when they're not around can be a sign of how much they're loved. This tends to be used as an excuse for backbiting, too, but, well, as far as I could see, this was within the scope of friendly playing.

Yukinoshita and Yuigahama are both adored by their juniors, huh?

As I was pondering these matters, the electric kettle eventually made bubbling sounds, and the water started to boil.

Kettle in hand, Komachi hummed as she poured out the tea. A familiar aroma gradually wafted into the air, rising along with the steam.

While that was steeping, Komachi set out my Japanese teacup and two paper cups. It seemed she wasn't going to use Yukinoshita's and Yuigahama's cups, even though they were absent.

Holding the teapot in her hands, Komachi briskly poured the black tea into the cups—she was hardly green at this, after all (ha-ha).

"Okaaaay, here you go," she said.

"Ohhh, thanks." I raised the offered cup above my head in gratitude, then took the first sip. *Mm, I'm feeling great today, and the tea is, too...*

So I was enjoying the tea as usual, but Isshiki wasn't reacting so well. She took one sip, then another, squinting and scrutinizing the surface of the tea in the paper cup as if checking something. "Hmm..."

Isshiki's meaningful sigh made Komachi scowl. "Hmph! You have something to say? Is there some problem with it?"

Isshiki waved a hand at that. "No, it's fine... I was just thinking, Yukino sure is good at making tea, huh?"

"Ahhh... Yeah, compared with her..." Komachi's sigh sounded almost resigned, and she nod-nodded like that made sense to her, too.

But I wasn't about to do the same; I had a question mark above my head. "Huh? Does it taste that different?" I slurped another mouthful to let my palate examine its structure. I held it in my mouth for a while to check, but the taste spreading over my tongue was black tea. If she'd changed it to oolong tea or green tea, of course I would be able to tell, but black tea is always just black tea.

Huh... I don't get it at all... Is something different? I looked over at the one who'd made it.

Komachi shrugged with a wry smile. "It's the same tea leaves, but still..." Then she put a hand to her chin with a *hmm* and started to think. "Maybe it really does make a difference after all."

"Ohhh, did you change something?" I asked.

Komachi smiled vaguely. "You know, 'cause love is the secret ingredient."

Hmmm! That makes it sound like there's no love in this teaaa!

Well, it's true that just now, Komachi poured the tea in a quick, offhand, and almost careless manner. I'd been admiring her efficiency due to experience... Could it be there's no love in her regular cooking?

So I found myself doubting Komachi's love, but Isshiki shot that down. "No, no, it's just a different technique. Yukino puts a lot of time and effort into it."

"Hmm... Really...?" I tried thinking back on when I'd seen Yukinoshita pour tea, but I couldn't quite remember how much time she'd taken on it. Well, I think all her gestures are careful, not just when she makes tea, so maybe she's just refined in general...

But someone with an eye for it probably would see a difference.

Paper cup in hand, Isshiki took another drink. "When Yukino makes it, it's like, *Black tea!* But Okome-chan's feels like, *Tea...* It tastes like what you drink at home."

"You don't have to say it like that...," I grumbled. "Except I kinda get what you mean." I do drink Komachi's tea regularly, so it tastes exactly like home to me. Put nicely, it's simple and reassuring, I suppose...

Since she wasn't being explicitly dissed, it seemed Komachi didn't quite know how to react to these comments about her work. "But, like, isn't that more about your mental image of the tea…?" she said, frowning.

Isshiki nodded. "Well, that's part of it."

"Komachi can't do anything about that, though…" With a dry laugh, Komachi acquiesced. She was shrugging like Tora-san going, *If you're gonna tell me that, it's over.*

Well, we're a house of common plebs after all… You can't avoid the sort of humble domesticity apparent in not only the taste, but the way Komachi moves and comports herself. You can't compare that to the Yukinoshita family, with their air of high society.

But that humble housewifeyness is Komachi's charm, and that's precisely what makes her the little sister of the world.

It seemed Isshiki understood that without me having to make such arguments, as she was nodding like *Huh, uh-huh* and going "Wellll, I guess."

But then something must have struck her, as the motion of her head suddenly stopped.

Then she turned her whole body toward Komachi and swished the hair off her shoulders with the back of her hand.

Uh, your hair isn't long enough to swish off with your hand… Hey, wait. Is this déjà vu? I was thinking when Isshiki swished her hair a second time, then a third, and put that same hand to her temple. Then she breathed an exasperated sigh with a light shake of her head.

"My, that's not at all the case, is it? Komachi, if you must imitate me, I would prefer it if you could also imitate my manner of making tea." Isshiki's lips were wide in a smile that communicated absolute smugness.

Komachi and I both instantly snerked. Trying to hold back my laughter made a really weird sound.

Komachi failed in the end. "Wee-hee-hee!" But then after some time giggling, she wiped the corners of her eyes and offered her compliments to Isshiki. "That was good, Iroha! That's so her; it really is!"

Isshiki proudly puffed out her chest. "Heh, right? The key point for Yukino really is the smugness."

"Don't call it smugness..." She doesn't mean it like that.

...I *think*, but I dunno. That girl sometimes gives you the sense that she's reeeally enjoying letting you have it. Not that I hate it, really. I'd even say I find it pleasant, so I would like to continue humbly receiving her smugging in the future as well. I'm sure that smugness is part of why these two love her, too...

Meanwhile, said pair were both swishing their hair, jerking their chins away, and smiling smugly for their imitations. *Oh, now they're really enjoying themselves.*

Eventually, the impression contest seemed to end with Isshiki's victory. Komachi applauded her and gave her a big nod as if to say, *Some fine work there.* "Y'know, impressions really are more on point when they're malicious. Komachi would expect no less."

"I'm not being malicious!" Isshiki argued fiercely, smacking the desk.

Komachi stared back at her, cocking her head. "Really?" She was looking at Isshiki with innocence too pure to be genuine. Unconcealable delight flickered deep in her eyes.

"Really! Honestly, what do you take me for...?" Isshiki groaned and narrowed her eyes at Komachi.

But Komachi didn't seem to care in the least, putting one hand to her cheek as she twisted around coquettishly. "Huhhh?" she drawled in a sickly sweet tone. "But, Irohaaaa, aren't you aaaalways like that? Personally, I think maaaaybe it could fit you."

"That right there, that's a malicious impression. Hey, look, this girl's sense of ethics is totally broken." Isshiki turned to me to protest. And yet a single glimpse of that impression, which was supposedly nothing like her, was enough for her to recognize herself in it. She disregarded it as if to say, *Feh.*

But it seemed that was a satisfying reaction, in Komachi terms, as Komachi was happily tittering *eh-heh-heh. Oh, maybe she's glad Isshiki got her impression? Aw no, what the heck, how precious is that… Now this exchange feels kinda heartwarming…*

"Yeah, yeah, the malicious ones really are on the money!" she cheered.

…Or so I thought, but no, she was full of evil intent!

Komachi sighed in satisfaction, like, *I got her there!*

"I'm telling you, it's nothing like me…" Isshiki sighed in mixed exasperation and resignation. Then she glanced over at me. "It's not, right?" she asked.

"Nope," I answered with confidence. "Not enough cunning. Needs more cunning," I declared emphatically.

"That defense is not encouraging…" Isshiki's shoulders drooped in dejection.

Hey, but I was trying to sound really convincing, though…

"And hey, I'm not cunning or manipulative or whatever," Isshiki said, pouting as she jerked her face away.

"Uh, you're doing it right now… Wow, unbelievable… Is she doing it unconsciously…?" said Komachi. Her voice was filled with astonishment—even shock.

But I'm forced to say that view is a little shallow.

Clearing my throat with a little *hnn*, I laid my elbows on the desk in the Gendo pose and spoke in a low voice. "You've got it wrong, Komachi."

Perhaps because my tone was so serious, Komachi and Isshiki both looked at me with a start. Their gazes were both somehow tense and anticipating. With their attention on me, I continued with incredibly weighty, grave importance. "Isshiki is fully aware she's being manipulative. But that isn't all she is. While she builds on a foundation of cunning, that's not the highlight, and there's a certain kind of defiance to it. She's like, *I know I'm being manipulative, but this is me, okay…*" I stopped there, and after a full pause for effect, I finished the monologue. "…It's what you would call a cunning that isn't fawning," I said with a smiling sigh, and a moment of silence fell.

Then Komachi said, sounding totally weirded out, "Whoaaa, he makes a whole speech about it... But it's not like he's way off base, so we'll say it's fine." Apparently satisfied, she gave a couple of big nods.

"Right? That's what's nice about Isshiki," I said.

"I get it, I get it. She goes all out being cutesy, which is cool."

"Exactly."

Unexpectedly, Komachi and I wound up holding a "Competitive Presentation on What We Like About Iroha Isshiki."

There's so many other things, you know! Nice things about Irohasu!

All right, then I wonder what card I should draw next! Her looks go without saying, and mentioning that to her face would be super-embarrassing, too. If I was going to lavish her with praise to make fun of her, I wanted to go more for her inner attributes and spirit. So I guess it's gotta be that; her unique way of getting close to you is nice. She'll completely ignore those she's disinterested in but then come talk to you once she gets used to you, bringing a joy like encountering a wild animal.

I was about to lecture about such matters at length, but I was cut off by a tug on my sleeve.

I looked over to see Isshiki, face downturned and trembling. "U-um... Please stop... That is really embarrassing and I actually totally noway... And, like, it's not even true...," she muttered rapidly, cheeks bright red. Then she fanned her face with a palm and sighed. Since her eyes were on the floor the whole time, I got a good view of her pink ears peeking out from her pale hair.

Seeing her get genuinely shy about direct compliments is so precious..., I thought, and I couldn't help but observe it closely.

It seemed Komachi was the same way. She must have been trying to get a good look at Isshiki's response, as she was leaning all the way forward to peer at her face.

Isshiki jerked even further away.

"Tee-hee-hee," Komachi tittered. "No, no, it is true. You're a wonderful person. No matter how others react, you stick to your own style... It's not easy to pull something like that. I actually respect it, in a sense. Wow, you really are cool…" Eyes closed, Komachi mocked her with excessive praise and apparent admiration.

"StopitstopitcutitoutOkome—" Isshiki desperately tried to stop her, but even when she grabbed Komachi's shoulders and shook her back and forth, Komachi showed no signs of relenting.

"You don't care what people say, even if they hate you! You're unfazed! You shrug off whatever anyone tells you! It's cool!" Komachi gushed with glee.

"Uhhh…" Isshiki was horrified and bewildered in equal measure. "I'm not unfazed, though, and I don't shrug it off."

But Komachi completely ignored her, thrusting a fist out as she sang further praises out loud. "The strength to not cave to peer pressure! Ignoring rumors and backbiting! Iroha is so great! Mesmerizing, inspiring!"

"Whoa, no, I get hurt like anyone else when people hate me! Rumors and backbiting and stuff like that really get me down." Isshiki was waving her hands hard in front of her chest as she denied absolutely every compliment.

But Komachi, dreamy and entranced, touched a hand to her chest and closed her eyes so she couldn't see as she continued, "Komachi has always thought that you're so cool all the time—being yourself, no matter what other people think…"

"Hold on? Stop characterizing me like that? And don't lead everyone to think it's, like, okay to hate me?"

"That's what Komachi respects about you."

"Okome, listen to me! I want people to like me. I want to be loved, okay? What is this? Do you hate me?" Isshiki asked sourly.

Komachi cocked her head. But then with utter nonchalance, she answered immediately, "In a sense, I actually fairly seriously kinda like that sort of thing about you."

She said it so blithely and so equivocally, Isshiki blinked two, three times. But eventually, it seemed she figured out what that meant.

Isshiki snapped her jaw shut and pressed her lips together, and then she started constantly fixing her bangs. "U-uh-huh...," she mumbled under her breath. "I see..."

Seeing her reaction, Komachi smiled brightly.

And then there was me, watching the two of them like *Huh...* with an unaffected, dapper, and kind of awkward smile.

But in my heart, I was sobbing from how precious it was. *Ohhh my, all aboard the SS KomaIro! Awww, Iroha-chan is normally such a teasing master, but now she's been bested by Komachi, another teasing master.*

Well, this was mostly just Komachi getting carried away teasing, but I don't think it was all entirely a joke. And she wasn't necessarily wrong, either. It's true that the way Isshiki sticks to being herself, however other people react, is cool.

On the other hand, as Isshiki herself said, hearing people saying things had to get her down. But I think what makes Isshiki cool is that even if she mopes, loses heart, and feels uncertain, in the end, she'll put on her cutest, most charming smile.

Oh no, at this rate, we'll wind up holding the second "Competitive Presentation on What We Like About Iroha Isshiki." I'll win this one for sure...

As I was all fired up and ready for a rematch, Isshiki cleared her throat as if attempting to cover her shyness as she pushed her paper cup forward. "...More, please," she muttered quietly. The paper cup was already empty.

Considering all she'd said about it being common or humbly domestic or whatever, she had in fact drunk all the tea Komachi had made.

Komachi smiled gladly. "Sure!"

And then, teapot in hand, she gleefully and diligently poured another, and Isshiki expressed her gratitude with a quiet "Thanks."

Watching this interaction, I was already starting to consider putting together an organizational committee for the third "Competitive Presentation on What We Like About Iroha Isshiki."

×　　×　　×

Once I was comfortably drinking tea and munching on snacks, I suddenly remembered something.

Because of that Service Club imitation show and the "Competitive Presentation on What We Like About Iroha Isshiki" and whatnot, we'd wound up having quite the mad tea party, but didn't Isshiki come here to do something?

"Isshiki," I said.

She was munching on one of the cookies we had to go with the tea, and she was just reaching out for another. "Hyeah?"

"Wasn't there some reason you came here?" I said, and her hand froze.

"Ah."

"Ah."

Both Isshiki's and Komachi's faces were saying, *I completely forgot...* Well, I'd completely forgotten, too, so I totally wasn't going to judge.

Isshiki withdrew the hand that had been reaching out for the snacks, then petted and flattened the wrinkles of her skirt, straightened her posture, and started over.

"If you *muuust* call it work, then yes, I did more or less come with work. There was a liiiittle something I wanted to ask you about..." She put her index finger to the end of her chin as she said exactly the same thing as she had before.

"Oh-ho? Then let's hear it." But this time, of course, Komachi didn't do an impression of Yukinoshita. Her expression was sharp and serious as she prompted Isshiki to continue.

Though Isshiki nodded back, her eyes were still on the seats of the two absentees, Yukinoshita and Yuigahama. "I'd actually prefer it if Yukino and Yui were here..."

"Then next time works. Next week, or the week after that, or after that. Right?" I looked over at Komachi, and she nodded back.

"...So my brother fully intends to put it off, but what will you do?"

"Hey? Can you not accurately commentate on my intentions?"

Aw geez! With my little sister in my workplace, my normal techniques for sneakily slipping out of things won't work. I don't know what to dooo! If she says something like that beforehand, then none of my prepared excuses will work, will they?

So I was thinking, but Isshiki seemed to not pay much mind to that, waving a hand in annoyance. "Oh, that's okay, that's okay. It's just the usual anyway."

Aw geez! It looks like none of my excuses would work, right from the start! Well, Isshiki's known me long enough, too, so unsurprisingly, she knew what I would say.

And Isshiki did have a composed little smirk on. "Besides, I know how to deal with him at times like these," she said, then cleared her throat experimentally, straightened in her seat, and scraped her chair across the floor to face me directly.

"Um...," she addressed me weakly, voice shaking slightly. A heated breath slipped from her pink lips, which were shiny with colored lip gloss, as she examined me with upturned, ephemerally moist eyes. "...We can't...do it?" she murmured hesitantly, her trembling fingers squeezing the front of her uniform. Her tone, gestures, and expression were all very emotional.

When she asks me like that, it's really hard to shoot her down...

As I was overwhelmed—hyperwhelmed, even—Isshiki did a full one-eighty and scoffed in utter contempt. "See, down in one shot." She puffed out her chest like, *How d'you like that?*

"Ohhh." Komachi clapped in applause.

But I could only say sourly, "No, you're underestimating me. I'm already used to that, and there's such a thing as being too obvious about it... I can clearly tell whether you're serious or not, at least."

Well, even if I am used to it, though, it's not like it doesn't get my heart racing! I thought, but I kept that to myself and scowled at them instead.

Then Isshiki totally flipped from her earlier elated smile, narrowing those big eyes of hers into a cool expression. "Huhhh." Her tone oozed skepticism, as if to say, *I dunno...* Then something apparently occurred to her, and she smirked enchantingly.

She reached out to grasp my cuff and tug me close. When I leaned toward her, she whispered softly into my ear, "...Are you sure you want me getting serious?"

Her voice was hushed, soft, and sweet—not just tickling my earlobes, but making me tremble to my spine. I bent backward away from her, and when I looked at her again, she pressed a fingertip to the bewitching smile on her glossy lips.

I shook off her examining gaze and just barely shook my head. "Stopstopyou'rekindascaringmeI'lllistensostop," I rattled off rapidly in an attempt to cover how she'd gotten to me.

Isshiki must have been satisfied by my reaction, as she released my sleeve, puffed out her chest with a smug chuckle, and offered Komachi a triumphant smile. "See?"

"You're so easy, Bro." Komachi gave me a condescending look.

No, you've got the wrong idea. There's nothing like that with Isshiki— it's just my ears, okay? My ears are a bit of a weak point... But if I were to expose my kinks as an excuse, that look of condescension would turn to contempt.

While I was busy escaping from Komachi's gaze, I took the opportunity to crack my neck and shoulders. "Anyway, what did you want to talk about, actually?" I asked, as if the exchange just now had never happened.

Isshiki folded her arms to consider her wording, touching her hand to her jaw with a *hmm*. "Well, I'll leave the details for when Yukino and Yui are here, but for now, I'll just bring up the short version."

"Oh?" *I'm not sure I like how she phrased that...*

I've heard it's generally accepted in adult society that just the short version by itself is an unblockable death flag.

At first, they'll bring up something like *Do you have time next month? I might ask you for a favor. It'll probably be okay, though*, but then once it is later and you have no time, they'll suddenly shove in that item and get legitimately angry with you and be like, *I told you to open up next month, didn't I? …Or so I have heard.*

However, since I'd asked what she'd come for, I had to listen to this short version of hers. With just my eyes, I prompted her to continue.

Isshiki gave me a little nod and began. "The truth is, during summer vacation—"

"I'm not helping," I said, reacting so fast you'd think I was botting. *After seeing his footwork, it was easy.*

Komachi promptly flipped out. "Bro! That was fast! So fast! Probably anyone but Komachi would've missed a rejection that fast!"

Uh, I mean there's no way I can help during summer vacation… Did you not see that word, vacation? *Besides, I am more or less studying for exams. I can't be focusing on other things during the summer that will decide the rest of my life. Especially when I haven't done any exam studying yet!*

But Isshiki must have understood my rationale, as she readily agreed. "Oh, no, I don't really need help. I wouldn't send a third-year out during summer vacation; I'm not totally heartless." She was waving a hand in front of her chest like *No, no.*

Reeeeally? You're not heartless? "Oh, I see…" I eyed her doubtfully.

She huffed. "Really. I'm not even planning to send out the vice president."

"Huh…" *If even the chief of the Victims of Iroha Isshiki Association is getting exempted from labor, then it seems I can trust this a little bit… Now I can relax and listen.* "So what're you doing?"

"There's a school information session for prospective students. Well, the school admin will be putting on the info session, and the student council is just helping a little."

"An info session, huh…?" I made listening noises like *hmm, hmm,* but this wasn't ringing any bells. I turned to Komachi to confirm. "Did our school do something like that?"

Komachi's reaction was lacking. She tilted her head like *Hmm?* with her eyes pointed upward. She considered awhile but finally shook her head. "Dunno? Maybe…"

"Huhhh...? You were just studying to get into here, though..."

"Yeah, but I didn't go to the information sessions or anything... And hey, three years ago, you were trying to get in here, too."

"I don't remember that far back..." The only real memories I have from the summer vacation of my final year of middle school are of the summer courses at cram school.

And you know me—I'm such a deadbeat, I only took the exams for this school because it seemed like I could pass. There's no way I would drag myself to a try-hard event like an information session.

Well, if it was like the rumors I've heard about post-university employment, where participation in the info session is vital for entry, then I would be forced to go—or if it was like an internship, with some perk like a leg up in selection down the line, that's something else.

However, if it's just a formal function to explain things, then no thank you.

In the first place, few people will actually listen to explanations.

With home appliances and the like, most people will not read the user manual. It's commonly known that everyone just kinda fiddles with it for a while, then says something like *I see—I basically get it*, and about 80 percent of the functionality is wasted. And I am no exception there. I'm so bad that I only just found out yesterday that our drum-type washing machine has a mysterious "air iron" function. Oh look, another function I won't touch with a ten-foot pole.

It seemed Isshiki had already taken into account that we wouldn't care, as she shrugged in resignation. "Well, that's basically about the size of it. I've never attended, either. It mostly seems like it's for the parents..." She let out a big *agh*, then shrugged again as if to say, *Good grief.* "But it seems like some middle schoolers are coming, so we have to prepare for that."

"Prepare? Are you gonna put something together?" Komachi asked, blinking her big baby eyes.

Isshiki nodded as if she found this all a hassle. "We talk about what the school's like, and then, well, some kinda tour where we actually look around the school buildings… Also taking questions and stuff?" she said, thinking over each item with a finger on her chin. It seemed the specifics hadn't been entirely firmed up yet.

Making lazy interjections, I listened until I had a vague outline of this school information session.

When she brought up the school tour, that one thing in particular made it easier to imagine.

To a middle schooler, I'm sure even just entering a high school building would be a little bit of an event, so that would actually make them happy. At the very least, if I were a middle schooler, I think that would legit get my heart racing.

Let's try imagining it a bit. Imaginate and calibrate.

—*Summer vacation.*
In the seething heat, the rising air shimmers over the asphalt.
The pleasant sound of metal bats ringing out in the distance, the loud buzzing of cicadas.
The school, on the other hand, is completely silent and undisturbed.
Not a soul can be seen inside. The hallway is entirely quiet.
A casually worn summer uniform, a thin skirt.
A cute older girl walking ahead.
During the school tour, when she asks why I'm choosing this school, I answer, "'Cause it's closest to my house." She laughs in exasperation, saying, "Whaaat?"
But then, when we part ways…
…she gently tugs my sleeve and touches my shoulder.
"…I'll be waiting," she whispers and smiles—

………*Yeah, that's nice. Nice. Can I join that tour, too?*
Without letting any of all that on my face, I *hmm*ed as if to say, *Oh yes, I was very, very deep in deep thoughts.* Oh, that's nice… Very nice… Hmm, nice…

"So in other words, it's, like…basically an open campus?" I said.

"Ah, that's the idea." Isshiki jabbed the finger that had been resting on her jaw at me.

I see. Call it an *open campus*, and I can get the picture.

Well, even if some teachers made impassioned speeches from the podium of the gym or auditorium or whatever to explain this and that, I doubt middle schoolers would actually listen. Maybe the parents would.

Third year of middle school—in other words, fifteen years old—is the age when you race out on a stolen bike and go around breaking the windows of the school at night. Which means guiding them around the school building and telling them where the most breakable glass is should really draw interest to our school.

As it was all coming together in my head, Komachi, diagonally across from me, clapped her hands. "Ohhh! Open campus! Now that you mention it, Komachi's heard of that before…" She suddenly folded her arms and gave a little *mmg*.

Isshiki looked at her sharply. "You know about those, Okome-chan?"

Komachi responded with an incredibly heavy nod, then flipped through the notebook in her hands. "Yes. Open Campus, the magic words that open a notebook…"

"I'm not talking about the brand name." Isshiki immediately waved a dismissive hand with a serious look.

Her cold treatment made Komachi stroke her cowlick as she giggled a little *eh-heh-heh* as if to say, *Yeah, of course*.

Aw, nooo! That Komachi-chan, she's such a jokester! She's cute, so I'll totally forgive her, but if she were saying that sincerely, I would've made her write out a real earnest essay of apology in that Campus-brand notebook. ☆

"Well, I do have a vague idea. Though not what it is specifically," Komachi said as she glanced over at me. Her gaze was seeking an explanation, like *But what does it all meeeeean?*

So be it. I shall explain for your sake.

"An open campus is…well, in plain terms, a school tour event at a university or technical school. They have trial classes, you sample the school cafeteria, and they show you the research labs and stuff...and introduce you to clubs? Apparently," I said.

Komachi gave me a smattering of applause. "Ohhh, as expected of a third-year."

"Well, you know." I flashed her a cool smile, but I haven't actually gone to one, either.

Man, once you get to your third year of high school, discussions around you tend to turn to entrance exams, so stories like that float your way. You know those people, the ones who will tell you in sordid detail about stuff like *I hear the open campus from such-and-such a place is good* or *I hear the commerce department will be interesting this year* or *But more importantly, did you know about the urban legend of that school?* Or maybe that's just the male friend character in dating sims.

When I showed off my limited knowledge on the subject, Isshiki made listening noises like *hmm-hmm.* "Well, a trial class or sample lunch is obviously out of the question. I'm thinking maaaaybe we'll do a general school tour, plus introduce the clubs."

"Hmm... Isn't that enough? Not like I know," I said.

"Whoa, you sound like you don't care...," Komachi said with a dejected look.

But there wasn't actually anything else I could say. For one thing, the keener type who would bother coming to a formal-sounding event like a school information session would obviously be happy no matter what you did. And then a cute older girl doing the tour and club intro and all that would thrill the boys, and the girls would see her as a role model.

So I honestly was taking an optimistic outlook, like *So, well, isn't that fine?* But Isshiki wasn't so happy. Curious, I shot her a look asking, *What's up?*

Isshiki sighed hesitantly with a mildly troubled expression. "So I have to make up a pamphlet introducing those clubs..." She paused there, flicking a glance over to Komachi for just an instant before turning back to me to finish. "But what do we do about the Service Club?"

"Why're you asking me...?" I reflexively avoided the question.

Despite Isshiki's wry little smile, earnest seriousness lay in the depths of her gaze. With her eyes fixed on me, I was forced to consider what she meant by that question.

This probably wasn't just about work.

I got the feeling she was asking what we planned to do about this club in the future, down the road.

The image I'd envisioned when I'd arrived at the clubroom that day rose in my mind again.

The following year, or a year and a half from now.

A girl reading a book in the slanting light of the sun.

The sight of Komachi, left behind alone in this room.

If I wanted to avoid making that fiction real, it would be best to tout the club to the new students.

But I wasn't the person to be asking about that. Komachi had been the one to take on the care of this club, of this place. We had accepted that this thing would inevitably end, and she had inherited it for us.

I was just the recipient of her blessing.

Though I was slightly anxious that this might keep her tied down.

I looked over to see Komachi scratching vigorously at her head as if at a loss. "Ahhh... Who knows... Komachi hadn't been thinking about it. For the moment, though...," she said, with an examining glance at me. That was about the same as what she'd told me before when we were alone together. Though she didn't bring up any concrete pros and cons, the evasive way she spoke suggested that she was leaning toward no.

If Komachi wanted to put it off for a while, then I would take over from here. I specialize in deferral, putting things off, and procrastination. "Do we have to put something in that pamphlet?" I asked.

Isshiki furrowed her eyebrows, considering with a *hmm*. "This is supposed to be an official club, more or less, so I think it's kinda sketchy to not mention it. The school admin will probably check it, too, so..."

"I see..." Any document being handed out at a school information session had to be checked by the school.

If the club wasn't in the pamphlet despite existing as an official club, then it was plenty conceivable that would be pointed out, and they would come to check.

If we weren't going to put it in, we would need an appropriate rationale.

The activities of the Service Club were fuzzy and dubious, after all.

If we drew attention to ourselves, then the school was bound to find it suspicious. It was bad enough that even I, a member, still wondered what the heck the Service Club was. To avoid future trouble, it would be best not to give them excuses to dig into it.

So I was racking my brain like *All right, so what do I have to do to sneakily slip out of this one?* when Isshiki let out a light *phew*.

"Well, I wouldn't say it's a rush, so if you could just think about it," she said, then looked at the empty seats.

Komachi's eyes were on the same spot. "All right. It's a bit difficult to decide only on Komachi's discretion, so we'll try talking with Yukino and Yui tomorrow." She clasped her hands into fists in front of her chest to pump herself up. *Zoi!*

This would affect the future of the Service Club. Yukinoshita and Yuigahama would also have their own thoughts about it. I had some, too. Whether I was going to put those into words or not, we should have the opportunity to communicate them.

So then, deferring a conclusion until tomorrow..., I thought, and I suddenly realized something.

...Tomorrow?

"Uh, tomorrow's kinda eh. I won't be here," I said, and both girls went blank-faced at the exact same moment. They cocked their heads in opposite directions.

"Oh, really?"

"Did you have something?"

"Prep school tour. And a trial class, too," I said with some smugness. *I may not look it, but I am studying for entrance exams, you know.* Although it was pretty late now to still be choosing a prep school.

The both of them made totally apathetic *huhhh* and *ahhh* noises.

"Huhhh, really?" said Isshiki. "Well then tomorrow Yukino and Yui will be in attendance...so maybe I'll pop in then."

"It's been a while since it was just us girls!" The two of them chattered cheerfully together.

At this point, I had an unfortunate announcement to make.

"Uhhh... Um, Yukinoshita also might not come?" I said, my gaze sneaking away in spite of myself.

It's not like I had anything to feel guilty about...and yet I was assaulted by such intense embarrassment that I could die.

There must have been something real funny about that, as Komachi and Isshiki both went "Mumu!" like the Rakuten Card Man, attention fully on me.

"Ah, that's what it is..." Eventually, Komachi seemed to figure it out, nodding *oh-ho, oh-ho* with a spreading warm smile.

Isshiki, on the other hand, wrinkled her nose in protest and let out a big, fat sigh. "Ah! There it is. Using the prep school tour as an excuse for your crap date."

"Don't use that language...," I said, scandalized. But I couldn't exactly tell her off because whether it was a date or not was yet to be resolved. Yes, hello, that's me.

×　×　×

There are a lot of things like trial classes or free tryouts out in the world, but not all of them are made with good intentions.

There are many unexpected pitfalls. For example, subscription services that declare the first month free, but if you read the contract carefully, they'll casually stick in the condition that you have to continue for two months or more; or if you apply for some supplement that says, like, "Act now and you get a free gift," then you'll never find the cancellation page for your whole life and they'll just keep sending it to you. You can apply so easily online, but then you have to cancel over the

phone. What's up with that? Thanks to that, we've got a lifetime sup-
ply of some supplement my dad ordered that's, like, supposed to be an
amazing combination of soft-shelled turtle and black vinegar and something something. This stuff is gonna make the turtles go extinct soon,
come on.

As they used to say way back when:

Nothing is more expensive than free.

Free services will generally have a catch. The free service exists
because there is some return exceeding the sunk cost in some form, and
someone, somewhere, is losing out. The turtles are getting saddled with
the risk of extinction, after all.

That's exactly why, even if it's just a prep school tour and trial class,
I make sure to read though all the detailed regulations in the school
brochures they give you. I read them deeper than textbooks or reference
books.

From what I've read of such material, what with the unstoppably
declining birth rates of our times, any prep school these days will have
enacted various policies for gaining new customers.

At the prep school I was touring that day, aside from having regular
lecture-based classes, they also incorporated a generous and courteous
support system, with online classes, archived class videos, and an associ-
ated smartphone app for academic help and whatnot, as well as mentors
attached to each individual for whatever.

Checking over all that stuff with the staff and asking questions ate
up quite a lot of time. So by the time I left the prep school, the sun had
completely set.

That's not good—I've gotta hurry, or I'll leave her waiting…

We were taking different classes. And then, if you considered the
time after that for asking them questions about the tour and such, we
would be leaving the prep school at different times. So it would be natural for this to move to meeting somewhere else afterward… Although
the conversation we'd had trying to figure out whether we would do so
had felt incredibly unnatural.

Regardless, we'd decided we would be meeting at a café that was pretty close to the station.

I headed there at a trot.

The café windows were west facing, so at sunset, they had the blinds inside the window lowered to keep you from seeing into the shop from the outside.

But I had the feeling she would be at the back there, waiting and reading a book.

When I entered the café, it was just as I had imagined, and I found Yukinoshita in a corner at the back, quietly turning a page in her paperback.

She looked hazy under the indirect lighting and the evening sun peeking through the blinds, just like a painting. Even though she was just sitting and reading a book, the girl called Yukino Yukinoshita was picturesque.

I'd seen a very similar scene before.

But one thing about her now was very different.

Her lips were split in a smile, and her eyes tracing the characters were gentle.

The feeling I'd had back then that she was hard to approach, that if I were to step into that space I might ruin it, was no more.

I quickly ordered just a coffee at the counter register and headed for that seat.

"Sorry for making you wait," I called out, and Yukinoshita popped up her head.

Then she smiled softly. "Oh, no. I only just arrived," she said, closing her book and tucking it into her bag. But her royal milk tea on the table had gone cold, and it looked like its volume had significantly decreased.

When she saw me observing the cup, she cleared her throat quietly as if to distract from that and picked it up for a sip. "My class was pushed back a little... You too?"

"The class ended on time. But there was a bunch of stuff I wanted to check—what it's like studying there and scholarships and stuff."

"Hmm…" She let out a sigh of deep interest before suddenly giggling. She was amused, but I had no idea what was so funny about the exchange we'd just had.

"What?" I asked.

Yukinoshita gave her head a little shake, but she was still smiling like it was funny. "Oh, no. This conversation is just making me think of university."

"University? How?" *What's with your image of university? You don't think it's just unbalanced because the sample closest to you is your big sister? Does she actually go to university?*

When I gave her a questioning look, Yukinoshita folded her arms and said, "Well…" Her gaze shifted up and to the left as she considered. "This is just how I imagine it, mind you, but…," she began, before continuing in a dreamlike murmur, "…I think it's meeting up after classes. Like, taking different lectures and then talking in the cafeteria after… I thought it might be something like this."

"Ahh, I get it…" Now that she put it like that, I could see how this was similar.

In that imagined vision, we wouldn't be in school uniforms anymore, and there was no timetable decided by someone else.

In the clothing we'd chosen, taking the classes we'd chosen, we were spending our own free time in the cafeteria together.

Our expressions would probably look more grown-up than now, but we'd be having the exact same conversations.

I wanted to see that, too.

But I also assumed I wouldn't.

"…Well, if we go to the same school, maybe something like that could happen. Not likely," I said with a dry laugh.

Yukinoshita looked huffy. "This is just a fantasy, so it's fine, all right…? You can be so pointlessly realistic sometimes, Hikigaya."

And you can be so pointlessly romantic sometimes… But I figured if I said as much, that pout of hers would get even poutier.

But her lips stuck out anyway, and she flicked her gaze away sulkily.

"...Besides, you still don't know. We're taking exams for similar institutions after all," she muttered in a teeny-tiny voice before looking at me for confirmation.

We were going in slightly different directions: Yukinoshita was going for public liberal arts while I was going for private liberal arts.

I'd given up on sciences from the start, so I wasn't going to take any public exams, but Yukinoshita would probably be applying for more than one school, and she would also apply for some private ones. There wasn't a zero chance we'd go to the same school.

But that was ultimately talking about possibilities.

No matter how hard I tried, I'd never get accepted into a national public university, and Yukinoshita wasn't going to go out of her way to come down to my level to choose a school... Right? If she went that far, that wouldn't be making me happy; it would just be scary. If that happened, I would do everything I could to stop her.

...But imagining her waiting for me at the cafeteria does kinda get me right there. Even today kinda got me right there.

So if I were to choose a plan of compromise...

"Well...it's all the same, either way. Even if we go to different schools, I'm sure we'll see each other," I said, rubbing my jaw as I pretended to think, hiding the smile that threatened to spread on my cheeks. I hoped we would do that, even if I couldn't know what would happen next year.

Yukinoshita looked at me closely in response, as if trying to decipher my true intentions. But eventually her pout broke into a smile. "Yes...we will." That nod was somewhat more innocent than usual; it made her seem soft.

But then she immediately giggled, and her usual indomitable smile rose to her face. "Although that's only if you don't fail all your entrance exams."

"Could you not target the exact thing I'm most anxious about?" *Seriously and unironically, that one isn't even funny...*

Well, my parents' policy is "We're not letting you take an extra year to study; go wherever you can get in," so even if I wanted to, I probably couldn't. So then I had to dedicate myself pretty seriously to studying for entrance exams. *Wahhh… Once you fail, you can't crawl your way up again. Japanese society is too scaaaary…*

As I was literally shaking and crying in terror, Yukinoshita shrugged in exasperation. "If you're doing that badly, I'm surprised you were interested in asking about scholarships."

"That's an important source of funds for me," I said.

Yukinoshita gave me a little nod. "Ahhh. You did say something like that in the past."

Some prep schools have a system where they partially exempt class fees to students with excellent grades as a "scholarship." If I could get that, then the difference between tuition and the money I got from my parents would all go in my pocket. This is the birth of the Full-Wallet Alchemist.

Well, that hurdle goes way up once you're in third year, and with everyone else hitting the books, it'll be difficult…, I thought with a sour sort of look.

Concerned, Yukinoshita asked me, "Are you struggling that much with money?" She was looking at me with such worry, eyes all dewy and eyebrows in an upside-down V like she might pull her wallet out that minute… I kinda felt like I'd become her sugar baby.

Hmm, this is actually not bad. No, it is bad—in terms of comfort level and social reputation.

I cleared my throat with a *gfem, gfem* to briskly cover up that discomfort. "If I have any problems, I'll borrow from my parents. Worst case, I'll get a job. If it's an ultra-short-term one-day contract, then, well, it should work out somehow."

As I rambled with my random nonsense, Yukinoshita sighed in mixed relief and exasperation as she lightly pressed her temple. "So getting a job is the worst-case scenario…" Then she looked up as if she suddenly had an idea. "…You could work for us? I think it would pay better than an ordinary part-time job."

"Ha-ha-ha-ha, absolutely not."

I'd heard Yukinoshita's family managed a civil engineering and construction-related company, but even if she suggested I work there, I didn't know what I would be doing, specifically. Was it just normal blue-collar labor? Wait, wait, this was the Yukinoshita family. The real big unknown wasn't what I would do, but what I would be made to do.

I didn't know what their official corporate structure was or anything, but Mamanon was functionally at the top, right? Just that alone would be workplace harassment…

Besides, I very much doubted Papanon would approach me favorably, either. I still hadn't met Papanon, but a guy who got anywhere near his dear daughter had to be a target for expulsion. If I were Yukinoshita's father, I know I would kill any boys who approached her.

And so I politely refused her offer. But Yukinoshita wasn't offended, putting a hand to her chin to consider. "I see… I thought it was perfect timing, though…"

I was a little scared, so I couldn't ask, *What? What timing?* So I decided to change the subject. "Well, I'm not really counting on getting a scholarship anyway, but then there's, like… Other than that, there's the issue of the environment. Location, facilities, support system, and everything else…," I grumbled.

After some deep consideration, Yukinoshita suddenly turned her face toward me. "Are you going to be selecting a different prep school? I thought the one we saw today was good…"

"Ah, no, it's not like I have any complaints. I just want to look into alternatives for comparison. Well, when it comes to quality of instructors—frankly, you can't really tell without taking a whole year's worth of classes, so that means you compare other stuff," I said.

Yukinoshita cocked her head. "By *other stuff*, do you mean the size of the independent study rooms, or the amount of reference material?"

"Well, that, too, but… Hmm," I said.

The size of study rooms and the number of chairs is indeed important. When it's too crowded and you can't get a seat even when you came in eager to study, you wind up in a mood for the whole day like *Oh, come on!* I'm also very grateful to have reference books and past problems to borrow.

But that only matters if you actually have the drive to go to the prep school in the first place. If it's too far, you won't feel like going, and it's also best to avoid places with a lot of temptations, like arcades and such. When you get down to it, entrance exam studying hangs on your ability to eliminate various excuses not to do it.

So you should choose a location that makes it easy to manage your motivation. If you think about it that way, the items you should prioritize decide themselves.

"…Number one is having a restaurant with good food nearby," I said.

As the ancient peoples have said, you cannot do battle while hungry.

Good food leads to motivation. Conversely, if the food is lacking in spirit, your motivation will be, too.

Mmm-hmm, that's right… I had convinced myself.

But Yukinoshita sighed deeply. "I'm sure the prep school won't expect to be chosen on reasons like that…"

"Hey, it's an important element in motivation management. For summer courses, you have two or three classes in one day, and then you're holing yourself up in a study cubicle on top of that, so you'll be there all day, right? Of course you'll be eating nearby. Food isn't just about simple replenishment of nutrients; it also means refreshment. So there's nothing better than to choose a school with a good restaurant in the area."

I firmly held back what I actually wanted to say, which was *But delivery is the real deliverance!* If I said anything stupid, she'd get exasperated with me.

So I thought. *Oh, that Yukinoshita. She's already annoyed with me!*

"The irritating thing is how incredibly convincing that completely hollow argument sounds…" She touched her fingers to her temple as if she had a headache, cheeks spasming in disgust. But suddenly, her cheeks relaxed, and she sighed gently in either exasperation or resignation. "…But it's true. I think I've never considered that."

"Right?"

Well, if you're choosing based on food, your problem gets to be that you're limited to what's near a good ramen place… And if I can be greedy here, too, it's even better if there's a sauna nearby as well. But maybe that really is asking for too much. You won't even know anymore if you're going there to study or to get sorted out.

As I was turning my thoughts to such wishes that would never be, Yukinoshita nodded. "Mm. Well then, which prep school will we be looking at next?"

"Huh? You're coming?" I asked without thinking.

Yukinoshita cocked her head with a blank look. "Are you not?"

"Uh, I am, but…" *I do plan to go see other prep schools… But you don't need to, do you? Right? Didn't you like the place we went to today?* I thought, and I'm sure this came across loud and clear in the way I trailed off and in the way my eyebrows came together dubiously.

When Yukinoshita realized, she let out an *ah* and covered her mouth. That hand gradually rose up to hide her cheek. Then she slid her gaze away. "I thought we would be going to the same school," she murmured hesitantly, her cheeks flushing beet-red.

But I couldn't bring myself to fire any comebacks at her. I was aware my own cheeks were on fire. "Oh, I don't mind if we're together, though… With these things, you've really got to consider taste and what suits you and what doesn't and stuff, not like I know," I mumbled.

While I got more and more flustered, Yukinoshita nod-nodded. That must have helped her pull herself together. She adjusted her seat, petting and arranging her skirt hem while she was at it, finger-combed the hair that came down over her shoulders, and corrected her posture.

Eventually, she began, "It's not as if I'm not considering it at all…" She sucked in a little breath, then began speaking more rapidly. "I feel your opinion of heavily weighting environment in order to maintain motivation is incredibly reasonable. Therefore, I believe I will also choose to weight environment heavily in my evaluation."

"O-oh, yes, indubitably..." *Why is she speaking weirdly formally...?* It made me give a weird answer, too.

"So then if I'm to consider the environment..." Up until then, Yukinoshita had been speaking as if this was all very well reasoned, but she stumbled.

When I asked with just my gaze, *What's wrong?* She gave a little shake of her head and muttered, "Umm..." like she wasn't sure how to put it, and she kept fussing with her bangs as she continued talking. "If I'm to consider the environment, um, I think I could work harder if we're together..." With a shy, bashful *eh-heh-heh* sort of smile, she combed her hair over and over.

Her usual reserve was gone; that smile was so incredibly innocent. I had no idea how to respond.

Is she for real...? Give me a break, seriously... I'm gonna turn into jelly with my head in my hands... Are you okay? Are your mental faculties alive? Yes, we are! *Phew. Looks like they were.*

So this means I've got no choice but to go to the same prep school as her, don't I? Wait, no. I can't do this. But I can't think of any reason to refuse. The only concern I have here is that I really don't think I'll be able to concentrate on studying at all; either way, I'll obviously be spending my time wondering what she's doing, so... Yeah, you could say it makes no difference where I am. In fact, I could avoid worrying unnecessarily, which means it would actually be constructive. Okay, excuse complete.

Firmly resisting any potential urge to smile, I put on a particularly weighty expression and nodded at her. "Well, you know, it is quite possible that after looking into a variety of schools for comparison, we would choose the same prep school in the end." But after getting that far, my attempt at a cool facade immediately flaked right off and fell away. "In fact, it'd probably happen; yes, I indubitably will do it." Maybe that earlier weirdness hadn't worn off completely.

That must have influenced her, too, as her nod in return was especially stiff. "Yes…that is my intention…"

And then both our gazes wandered around from embarrassment.

I blew at my long-cold coffee in an attempt to compose myself, while Yukinoshita rustled around in her bag as if to cover for being at loose ends.

We had nothing you could call real conversation during that time. Our eyes just met in occasional glances when we nodded at each other with shy, slightly crooked smiles.

What the heck is this…? It's super-embarrassing… I suddenly want to die!

Okay, then let's try to fix this with a topic change! I gulped down some coffee to sharpen my mind and my expression. "Oh yeah. Thanks for yesterday. For going out shopping for Komachi's celebration," I said, bringing it up as if I'd just remembered it.

Yukinoshita jolted and faced me again. With a small shake of her head, she smiled. "Oh, no, we were thinking we wanted to give her a little something, too. I should thank you. Sorry for leaving you to take care of the club yesterday."

This time, I was the one shaking my head a little. I hadn't done anything much. We hadn't gotten any requests or consultations or anything. It had just been me minding the place in their absence and chatting with Komachi and Isshiki.

There was just one thing that was on my mind, though.

Those thoughts must have shown on my face, as Yukinoshita cocked her head. "Did something happen?"

"No… Well, I guess you could say there was something…," I answered evasively as I wondered how to explain it.

The matter Isshiki had brought us the day before wasn't big enough to be called a problem. She'd ultimately just come to check something. I might have just been trying to find a problem.

So first, I should tell her only the facts, with my personal opinion omitted. "Isshiki's told us there's a school information session coming up. Because of that, they're apparently making some, like, club introduction material? And we were talking about whether to put us in," I said, keeping it brief.

Yukinoshita gently touched a finger to her chin and considered awhile. "That's an issue that will involve the Service Club next year and beyond. Since it is an official club, I get the feeling there'd be difficulties if we didn't put it in…" Her thoughts were basically the same as mine. "Well, if we're not going to be recruiting new members, we should be able to talk our way out of it somehow," she said and concluded with an *mm-hmm*. We were on the same page, then.

When you got down to it, there was just one question here:

What did we plan to do with the Service Club next year? That was all.

"What did Komachi say?" Yukinoshita asked me.

"She didn't seem enthusiastic about it."

"I see…," she said, then offered nothing else.

She couldn't say any more. Just like me.

I could have an opinion, but I couldn't make the decision. No, that was a cowardly way to put it. This was because I was unable to even offer my opinion.

If I'd said that I wanted the Service Club to continue, I'm sure Komachi would have respected that, regardless of her own desires. That's what's terrible about me—I twist things and put the responsibility on other people.

"The clubroom is larger than you might think. Though it didn't bother me at all last year…," Yukinoshita suddenly muttered in the silence. There was a hint of loneliness in her voice, as if she was worried for Komachi. Yukinoshita knew what it was like to be alone in that room.

Komachi would also be spending her time like that. Put in my own subjective terms, Komachi was being left behind in that clubroom. Maybe that was why it felt so desolate to me.

That scene I'd imagined back when Komachi and I were alone

together in that room was playing across my mind again—until a bright voice broke into my thoughts.

"...But I think it will fit lots of people." I looked up again to see Yukinoshita wearing a soft smile.

I couldn't quite digest what she'd said. My head tilted, and I responded with a look: *What do you mean?*

Yukinoshita puffed out her modest chest with mild pride, a triumphant expression on her face. "Though it may be odd of me to say this of myself—people came to that clubroom even when I was the club captain, you know? Yuigahama joined, too. With Komachi as club captain, they'll have plenty of business."

"I can't argue that... Particularly the *even when I was the club captain* part," I shot back with a dry *ha-ha.*

Yukinoshita giggled. "Right? I think some of those are sure to be valuable encounters, too," she said lightly, but with earnest warmth in her tone. Her gaze was peaceful, as if she were reflecting on this past year. And then her eyes softened a little shyly when she added at the end, "...Like us."

"You think? ...Yeah." Finally, I was fully convinced.

Maybe I'd been too fixated on our relationships.

No, it was fair to say I'd deified them.

Somewhere in my heart, I must have believed the current Service Club—in other words, the way we were right this moment, with Komachi included—was the ultimate, was the greatest, was perfectly complete.

If not, then I wouldn't have said Komachi was being "left behind."

I'd unwittingly taken my own environment as an absolute; that misdirected sentimentality was based on my own subjectivity.

Selfish. Arrogant. Shortsighted and narrow-minded. Just how far up his own ass is this guy? I think he's an idiot. I wanted to tell him to go and die for the next ten years.

Had our relationships ever been perfect?

No, absolutely not.

They had always been twisted, torn in some places, occasionally cut off with that thin connection persisting, stretching out between us even when we continued to go wrong. That was what I thought our relationships were.

And Komachi was sure to experience the same. She would have lots of encounters from now on, and those would lead into some of her own irreplaceable relationships. Though that was so completely obvious, my sentimentality had caused me to overlook even that.

What I should be saying to Komachi was not some attempt to shift responsibility to her, like *Just do what you want* or *You should decide yourself*, and of course not something so babyish and lacking self-respect as *I want you to continue the Service Club*. It was something else.

With that realization, I let out a long, deep sigh. It was a feeling like a fish bone dislodging itself from my throat.

"Thanks," I muttered from the corner of my mouth.

Yukinoshita swished her hair back and smiled. "You're welcome. Though I don't know what you're thanking me for."

I wasn't sure if she actually did understand or not, but if she would do me the favor of pretending she didn't get it, then I would play along. "Oh, I mean about that present. I was just thinking, that's a worry off my shoulders for the celebration."

"I see. That's good." With a cool smile, she brought her royal milk tea to her lips. I did the same, sipping at my cold coffee.

But that calm lasted for only a moment.

Gradually, Yukinoshita's eyes started to shift around. Then she nodded like she'd steeled herself and reached into the bag she'd been rustling around inside before. Clearing her throat with a cough, she began, "…Talking about celebrating reminded me…," and then she pulled out a cellophane-wrapped package. She let her head drop in a bow, then held it out to me cautiously, like she was feeding a lion.

"Here…," she muttered, voice trembling a little along with her hands. The shaking made it hard to tell, but it appeared the package was homemade cookies or something.

When I timidly accepted it, I found inside the bag checkerboard cookies, star-shaped cookies, and heart-shaped cookies, oh my! So many different types.

"As a celebration, or maybe anniversary, I suppose... But it's not a huge occasion, so I thought it might be the wrong idea to get something too expensive, so I considered lots of things..." Relative to her words per minute, the volume of information was just about zero.

So what is it, in the end? I get that the vibe here isn't asking me to taste-test or something (if nothing else), but this feels weirdly meaningful... It's not like it's my birthday, Halloween, Christmas, or Valentine's Day. There shouldn't be any special reason for me to get cookies...

When I stared at Yukinoshita like *Huh? What?* she sneaked her gaze away, brushing her bangs aside with her fingers, and continued in a hesitant murmur. "It's a little late, but...it's been...one month... As an anniversary," she said, and she flicked me an examining look.

"I see," I answered instantly and sharply with a serious expression, but in reality, my brain was gunning its engine.

This is the kind of thing where you can't ask what anniversary. No, this is the kind of thing where you must not ask... The only anniversary I know is Gundam's fortieth anniversary, but the one month *should be a hint.*

Hmmg, I considered as I stared at Yukinoshita, searching for that answer.

.........*It's so cute when she tries to hide her shyness.*

But such impressions flew right out the window when I realized the answer. I mentally blanched in panic.

When I reflected on the past month or so, there weren't many events to commemorate between Yukinoshita and me—however, the relative paucity of moments meant there was definitely one that stood out.

Tie that one event to the words *one month,* and the answer emerged on its own.

—This is what they call the "one-month anniversary."

Oh man...

So she's the type to do this stuff? Come on, tell me earlier! This is one of those things that will definitely lead to a fight if you forget. Like where you flee to a pachinko parlor and kill some time calming yourself down, then you have to buy her some makeup before you go back and apologize.

"...I didn't get you anything, though," I told her honestly. Even if I made some bad attempt at covering it, she'd see right through me anyway.

Yukinoshita shook her head. "I'm just doing it because I want to."

"Oh, okay… Well, that's still kinda like…" *Reciprocity is a thing, y'know? It makes me feel like I have to shape up, too, y'know?*

Seeing me flustered, Yukinoshita giggled teasingly. "You really don't have to worry about it. Oh, I know—so then let's say you'll do something for me next time."

"Next time… Oh yeah, next time, huh, next time…" Muttering "Next time, next time…" like I was in a delirium, I suddenly realized something. "When's the next time after one month? What interval do you do this at?"

I have no idea about this stuff… Will it come up if I Google it? Or would it be faster to look up a something-or-other anniversary sort of hashtag on Insta? But then I feel like you'd get a bunch of posts acting like every day is a special salad anniversary.

As I was worrying about this, it seemed Yukinoshita was also at a bit of a loss. "I'm not sure… I think any time is fine, though….But if you're going to do it, then perhaps a one-year anniversary is a solid choice?"

"One year…" *Ah man, I just can't imagine it at all. Even saying it out loud, it doesn't feel real.*

In one year, I would have graduated from high school and be right in the middle of a new lifestyle, but that scenario didn't quite click with me. Actually, by that time I would have managed to pass university entrance exams. If I failed, I think my future self would have come and killed me right here and now.

My future seemed so vague and distant, I couldn't even say anything. Yukinoshita must have taking that silence as bewilderment, or a rejection, as she hastily added, "I-is that too soon? Then maybe a…t-ten-year anniversary?"

"Te…" I stuttered on the exact same syllable that had momentarily caught Yukinoshita. *Whoa there, ten years…* Not even pro baseball players hear about contracts that long-term most of the time.

Even Yukinoshita must have thought it was too long a wait, as she immediately corrected herself. "Honestly, any time is fine… Don't worry about it too much…" Then she covered her bright-red cheeks and peeked out between her fingers.

The moment our eyes met, I held my head in my hands to hide my own cheeks.

Honestly, look… Is she for real…? Give me a break, honestly… Never mind ten years—I won't be able to forget this for decades… Are you okay? Are you alive, mental faculties? Hello? Brain? Hello?

× × ×

Well, it's not really something I have to worry about, but still…

I'm not a member of the club or anything, so I knew it wasn't like my showing up that day would resolve that discussion from the day before.

But even so, when I saw him and Okome-chan alone together in that big room, it put me in a mood to pop in for the heck of it. Well, I'd made up my mind to begin to pop in as often as I could when they were there, though, so whatever.

And so, once again, I'd shown up at the Service Club room.

This time, it was me, Yui, and Okome-chan.

With just the three of us, the clubroom really was just like the day before, but it looked somehow half-empty.

I'd like to quickly work out the stuff we talked about yesterday, though… I don't know if they're on a prep school tour or a crap date or what, but I'm pretty busy myself now that summer's coming, I thought as I glared at one of the two empty chairs lined up together.

Then I got curious about something. "Ohhh, wait. You didn't have to go tour any prep schools, Yui?" I plunged right in.

"Huh?" Yui, who'd been munching on snacks and guzzling tea like eeeverything was normal, jumped in her seat, then went back to munching.

"Ummm," she mused. She swallowed a gulp of tea, stroked her bun, and smiled awkwardly. "Wellll, I was wondering about what I should do…," she said with an evasive *ah-ha-haa*.

Seeing that, I sneakily whispered into the ear of Okome-chan, who was beside me. "She's moving to the defensive."

"You don't think her strategy is to deliberately take a step back…? Komachi's heard that the game isn't just about playing hard to get or getting ahead, but also about letting your opponent take a fake lead and cornering your mark," Okome-chan said as she nodded *oh-ho, oh-ho* with a know-it-all face.

The heck is this girl talking about…? I thought, giving her a sidelong glance.

Meanwhile, Yui stabbed out one hand to flatly argue, "No, that's not what it is. I was thinking maybe I could ask Hikki afterward and then go where he was going."

This time, Okome-chan brought her face closer to mine to whisper, "Isn't this an attack?"

"True…nothing's stronger than throwing out paper the instant your opponent plays rock…"

…Well, with that guy, if you ask him to teach you, help you, or give him a hand, he'll complain, but he will actually work things out for you. As expected of Yui. She's known him for a long time—yeah, she gets it, I thought, impressed.

Meanwhile, Yui was flailing and waving her hands. "No! That's not what it's about at all! I'm saying it'll be useful, since we'll be taking exams for the same sorts of places!"

"Oh, really?" Okome-chan's mouth popped open as she cocked her head quizzically.

"Yeah. I'm going for private liberal arts, so, well, probably mostly the same?" Yui answered, nodding, but then her head tilted to the side for some reason. This was about her own future.

Incidentally, I was also *hmm*ing thoughtfully. "Ohhh. So you're taking entrance exams, too," I commented carelessly.

"Of course I am!" Yui whipped back toward me. I worried she was going to break into whimpering tears. "Come on... Iroha-chan, do you think I'm that stupid?"

"No, no, that's not what I mean at all. I knew you were going to take entrance exams; I understood that. It's just, like, hearing about it struck me again...," I added hurriedly, sneaking my eyes away. Uh, not out of guilt or anything. I did think Yui was a little eh in the brains department, but honestly just a little...

And then, after averting them, my eyes landed on that pair of empty seats.

I probably hadn't just been looking away from Yui. I think I was unconsciously looking there, too.

Coming to the clubroom when they weren't there that day and the day before, seeing Okome-chan looking far quieter than usual, and hearing talk about a future where prep school and entrance exams had become concrete—the reality was sinking in.

They honestly were going away.

"Ahhh, yeah... So, I guess, until summer?" Yui said, her gentle voice not a reply to my flustered excuse, but maybe directed to the room she was gazing slowly over.

The stacks of desks, the swaying curtains, the wall clock that was a little behind, the abandoned Christmas debris in the corner, the blackboard with some faint, half-erased characters, the table with the tea set on it, the two empty seats side by side.

Yui gazed at each thing, and her eyes softened with fondness. Her glossy lips curved in just a slight arc.

Watching that mature smile, I gave a listless little sigh.

Whoa. I could even cry.

It totally wasn't even time yet for graduation or retiring from clubs or anything, but it felt like a weird switch was about to flip in me. Crying now would be a waste of tears, so instead, I let out a big *haagh*. *This is just such a hassle*, that sigh said, *I so don't have the energy*.

"Summer, huhhh. Then I guess it's like you'll just baaarely miss the school info session," I said, forcibly bringing up a different topic.

Yui cocked her head and asked me with her big eyes, *Is there something?*

"Oh, there's, like, this information session for middle school students who'll be taking our exams. There's going to be a school tour, and we, like, introduce the school clubs and stuff."

The beautiful and adult smile melted off Yui's face. "Ohhh," she said, nodding with her mouth hanging open dumbly. My moist eyes dried in seconds.

Since I'm here, might as well ask Yui.

This was an issue I had to deal with now, while they were still here. If I didn't, then I'd get tied up in the "now," then get caught in the past, and then she and I both wouldn't be able to go anywhere anymore.

I folded my arms with a *hmm*, tilted my head, and continued. "So we have to put together a pamphlet introducing the clubs, and we were talking about whether to put the Service Club in and what we should do with that. Right?" I turned it to Okome-chan beside me.

She was folding her arms in the same way I was, tilting her head. "Hmm, yeahhh. I wonder what we should do," she replied with zero sense of seriousness. It's not like I expected Okome-chan's answer to change in just one day, so that was fine.

When I looked over at Yui like, *What do you think?* she jumped on it with her answer.

"Why not—let's put it in. Let's get lots of new members," she said forthrightly, the words a certain guy had hesitated to say before.

I'd known she would say that.

Yui understood all the considerations and reservations that kept him and Yukino from saying things, thinking they were being kind, and then Yui deliberately pretended to be an idiot to say it out loud for them.

Okome-chan *hmmm*ed uneasily before shooting back with a strained smile, "In Komachi terms, I don't think we need to do any of that for a while, though... Komachi's got her hands full taking care of my bro."

"Ahhh. Mm, well, yeah, Hikki," Yui said, gently going along with that, though she smiled wryly in exasperation. I couldn't bring myself to smile.

Well, I'd figured Okome-chan would say something like that. She was playing it off as a joke, but that was probably pretty for real. She really couldn't think about new members right now, and it was true she was looking out for him in all sorts of ways.

So most likely, what Okome-chan valued was not the Service Club itself, but the Service Club as it was now. What she wanted to take care of was ultimately the space and time where they were. It was kind of like how I'd thought briefly that if the Service Club was going away, maybe they could do their stuff in the student council instead.

...Though I don't actually know what Okome-chan thinks about it.

The only one I know is myself, so there's nothing for it but to imagine based on my own standards—at least, that was how I used to think. I didn't want anything foreign in there, myself included. I don't think that at all now, and it's even like, I don't really care.

Still, I couldn't help but react when Yui softly said, "Hmm, but maybe someone will come and join...eventually..."

"Huh? You think?" I replied.

"Is there someone?" Okome-chan joined in.

When the two of us both jumped on that, Yui rapidly apologized, drawing away slightly. "Huh, oh, sorry, I have no idea. I was just kinda trying out saying it."

Whaaat, you were just saying it?! You made me get all excited... I sulked hard at Yui.

Then she clapped her hands and patched over what she'd said.

"Okay, but look, you don't know about the future, right? Anyone could just walk in, not just the new students. It was around this time when I joined in my second year. And Hikki joined around then, too."

"Now that you mention it, yeah…," Okome-chan acknowledged.

But I didn't know any of that, so I wound up reacting like *Huhhh, really?* I'd never heard about that stuff at all. The three of them were already there by the time I'd come to the Service Club, so I'd assumed they'd always been members.

Then Yui nodded as if to say *Right, right* with an easygoing laugh. "So I think it might become something like that… Like us," she said offhandedly. But…

"Ohhh, *like you guys* is frankly a little yikes, though," I said, waving my hands in front of my chest like *No way, no way*.

"Komachi's a little unsure, too…" Okome-chan's shoulders slumped dejectedly, and she gave a strained smile.

"Huhhh…? I meant it as a good thing, though…" Yui was tilting her head like *Ohhh? That's funny*. But she knew what I meant.

Relationships like theirs—overly complicated, ridiculously troublesome, and constantly going wrong—can't be built so easily. I mean, I don't even want that. No matter how hard I deliberately tangle things up, I wind up assembling way better, way more respectable relationships.

But they'll still probably go wrong somewhere along the line.

Maybe someday the two of us will find relationships like that. I'm sure of it.

With that thought, I glanced to the side, and our eyes met.

And we shrugged, sighed, and giggled softly.

X   X   X

It was after school, and the day was bright.

A peaceful air flowed through the clubroom. After two days away, all the members of the Service Club were now present, myself included.

The after-school melodies reached us on a balmy breeze, with the air of early summer coming in from the open window. I knew it couldn't change all that much in just a few days, but even so, the tones of the band club and the calls of runners felt somehow more in sync. Our mundane days were always continuously changing, bit by bit.

Even the clubroom of the Service Club was no exception.

The distance between our chairs, the length of a skirt, the number of words exchanged, the speed of turning pages—put measurements to any of these things, and they would just be petty differences, but they were clearly changing.

Of course, things that can't be expressed in numbers will change, too.

The greatest example was the brightness of Komachi's expression as she hummed and tappity-tapped on her smartphone. From my perspective as her older brother, it seemed like a weight had been lifted off her shoulders, compared with how she'd been two days ago. But this wasn't something that could be expressed in lux, candela, or lumens.

It was just a feeling.

Did that start last night? I thought, trying to remember, but unfortunately, my mental faculties had died the day before, so I couldn't think of anything. However, I had no recollection of seeing her in low spirits, so I inferred something had happened after school the day before.

But if you were talking changes, the one most changed in the clubroom right then was Yukinoshita.

Yukinoshita, who normally would have been done making tea already, had still not gotten around to the task.

This was because she had spent the whole time studying Komachi, then Yuigahama, nodding and shaking her head all the while.

This was all about trying to find the right moment for the surprise present for Komachi.

I understand that feeling. I do, but calm down a little. It's so fishy, and Isshiki seems suspicious. She's really staring at you. Maybe she doesn't like surprises?

Once it seemed like Isshiki was on the verge of asking *Um, what are you doing?* Yuigahama finally nodded at Yukinoshita a couple of times, giving her the go sign. Yukinoshita nodded triumphantly back as if to say, *Leave it to me*, swishing her hair off her shoulders. Then she rose to her feet and started to make the tea.

Without missing a beat, Yuigahama turned, chair and all, toward Komachi. "Komachi-chan, did you get a new hairpin? I don't think I've seen that one before," she said, drawing her attention.

"Ohhh? Really? Maybe 'cause it's one Komachi hasn't used in a while."

"Let me see, let me see. Can I fiddle with your bangs, too?"

"Go ahead, go ahead."

When Yuigahama beckoned, Komachi thrust her head toward her like a cat nuzzling you with one of those *purr-meows*, and before you know it, Yuigahama had expertly blocked Komachi's field of vision.

Oh-ho, not bad there..., I thought, impressed. Meanwhile, Yukinoshita deftly prepared the tea.

Eventually, the water in the kettle came to a boil, and she began gracefully pouring the tea with neat movements. The familiar aroma wafted around, and a faint steam rose up.

She lined up a Western teacup, a mug, a paper cup, and a Japanese teacup, and then beside that, she placed a chic little box. Isshiki watched her carefully open the box. "Ohhh, that's what it is," she whispered, flickering a momentary glance at Komachi, who was still in kitty mode.

"Isshiki...," I called to her quietly, and she glanced back at me. I gave her a little nod to say *Yeah, yeah, it's what you think it is* and touched my index finger to my lips.

From that gesture, Isshiki must have understood completely, as she slowly nodded without a word. She gently tucked her flow of hair behind her ear, then touched that same finger to her glossy lips with a wink. *Hmm, well, just nodding totally gets it across, so I'm okay here...*

As I was busy getting flustered, Yukinoshita finished making the tea and poured it into each of our cups. "Go ahead."

"Yeah, thanks."

The Japanese cup was placed before me, and the paper cup in front of Isshiki. Then there was Yuigahama's mug, the tea going to everyone in turn before, finally, to Komachi.

"Komachi. Go ahead," Yukinoshita said, and Yuigahama popped away from in front of Komachi.

"Oh, thank you very… Hmm? Huh? Ohhh? Hmm?" Komachi did a double take at the black tea placed before her, then a triple take, making strange noises. "Um, this…" She was pointing, confused, at a mug decorated with a wild strawberry pattern in white and pastel green.

When Komachi fidgeted like she was worrying about whether she could touch it, Yukinoshita answered her with a nod. "It's a bit late, but this is in celebration of your assuming the role of Service Club captain."

"And for remaking the Service Club. Thanks." Yuigahama smiled at her a little shyly.

Komachi looked between those two faces, then let out a breath. Maybe it was wonder, or maybe hesitation. "I-is this okay?"

"Yes," Yukinoshita replied. "It wouldn't look good for the club captain to be using a paper cup, now would it?"

"Yeah, use it kinda like—a proof of membership?" Yuigahama added.

At their urging, Komachi finally, gently touched the mug. She seemed to be testing the heat felt in her palm. Then she clasped it with nervous care in both hands. "Thank you so much…," she said, bobbing her head in a bow that didn't quite come up again. Then there was just the tiny sound of a sniffle.

Yukinoshita and Yuigahama looked at each other and exchanged gentle smiles. Isshiki was leaning her cheek on one hand, but her gaze was soft and approving.

I straightened in my seat and faced my sister. "Komachi." I made an effort to address her in a level tone.

Komachi slowly raised her head, scrubbing at her face with the back of her hand. Her eyes were wet, but she was looking straight at me.

There were lots of things I wanted to express to her, that I wanted her to know.

Like that I was proud, that I was grateful, that I was sorry, and everything else.

There were also matters related to her taking over, and maybe some kind of advice, too. I had too many anxieties, worries, areas of concern, and things I wanted to pass down to her to count.

The Service Club is frankly a hassle made up of overcomplicated types bringing in trouble. After our graduation, Komachi might have a bad time of it. She might feel lonely sometimes, too. I'm sure there will be times when she wants to give up. I wish it were possible for her to only experience the good times here, but I'm sure it won't be like that.

But I think including the good, the bad, the awful, the painful, the bitter, the frustrating, the sad, and everything else is what makes it the Service Club.

At first, you wonder, *What the heck is this club?*—but before you know it, you feel like it's hard to leave.

You think, *I could never do club stuff with someone like that*—but then you come to feel irresistibly drawn to them.

Nobody else could know, but just one person—just you—knows that sentimentality.

Maybe that's something you can get somewhere else, in any club, in any group of friends hanging out, but all I know is this place. Sorry, but I have no other way to get it across.

So at least, I want you to touch all of that, thoroughly and completely, with your own hands.

I couldn't say something like that succinctly anyway. I don't feel like just words would be enough to communicate it, and it's too embarrassing in front of everyone, so I kept all that to myself.

I smiled with just the corners of my lips, straightened in my seat like this was a matter of importance, and, with a silly gesture, bent my straightened back at a forty-five-degree angle.

"Then formally now, Captain Hikigaya: I'm honored to follow your leadership."

She stared at my silly bow; then she sniffed and laughed. "Ah-ha! Mm-hmm! Yes, you are!" Komachi puffed out her modest chest, putting on the most mannerly posture as she acted with as much haughtiness as she could.

Yuigahama, watching, nodded with a gentle *mm*, while Yukinoshita sighed in satisfaction. Isshiki, leaning her hand on her cheek, cracked an exasperated smile.

"Oh yeah. Speaking of thanks…" I glanced over at Isshiki.

At that signal, Yuigahama rustled around in her bag to bring out a stylish box. "Something for you, too, Iroha-chan. Thanks."

"O-okay… Thanks… Uh, you're welcome?" Though Isshiki couldn't seem to figure out how to answer, when Yuigahama handed her the box, she raised it over her head in thanks. "…Can I open it?"

"Go ahead," Yukinoshita prompted her.

After carefully peeling off the wrapping, Isshiki popped open the lid. When she saw the contents, she made a little sound. "Huh?"

Still with an expression of blank surprise, she pulled out what was in the box, placed it on the table, and examined it. Before her was a mug with a wild strawberry pattern in white and pastel pink. You didn't have to set it next to Komachi's mug to tell that it was the same design in a different color.

"Huh? Um, I'm not a member of the club, though… Is this okay?" Isshiki asked with some confusion and a shy smile.

"Oh, you weren't…?" Yuigahama muttered.

"Yeah, she's actually not. But for some reason, she comes all the time," Komachi whispered stealthily in Yuigahama's ear.

Beside her, Yukinoshita sighed in exasperation and shrugged. "Well, it's too late now. Besides, I don't like adding paper cups to the waste disposal."

Ohhh, I think I've heard that one before. Come ooon. For someone who

*doesn't like adding to disposals, you sure have a lot of excuses at yours ☆.
But if I say that, I think I would get beaten to a pulp, so I will keep quiet.*

Instead, I gave Isshiki a tiny bow. "Well, if anything happens, I'll
be counting on you."

Isshiki spent a few moments blinking at me, but she eventually
puffed out her not-so-modest chest with a smug chuckle that paid hom-
age to Komachi's earlier show. "Mm-hmm, yes, you will be... Don't
you think that was kinda...nonchalant? Weren't you being more polite
to Okome-chan?" Then when she realized what she was doing halfway through her reply, she got real huffy with a *hmph!* and heckled me
aggressively.

I was about to handle this by rattling off some nonsense like *Oh,
no, not at all. In fact, I have a reputation for being needlessly chalant about
a lot of things,* when from beside Isshiki, Komachi popped in and tugged
at her sleeve.

"Iroha, Iroha."

"What? What is it?" Isshiki answered as if annoyed.

Komachi swished back her blazer, flattened out the wrinkles of her
skirt, placed her hands on her lap, and did a dainty bow. "I am aware I
will be burdening you in many ways, but I formally ask that you please
take care of me in the future as well."

"Agh, well, likewise," Isshiki said, kind of confused at the sudden
polite bowing.

Taking advantage of her confusion, Komachi laughed with an *eh-heh-
heh* and barreled right on. "Also, for that thing you were talking about
before, please write up whatever sounds good! Komachi's leaning towards
putting us in ☆," she said cuuutesily ☆ and with the most crazily casual
manner possible. As in, Isshiki looked like she was about to lose her mind.

"So casual...and careless... Huh, I was kind of honestly worried
about that, though..."

At that, Komachi huffed out her nose, clenched both fists, and said
emphatically, "This is all because you were honestly worried. Oh, this
part is for real."

"Ah, I see... Not like I care anymore... Hey, your sister's sense of ethics is totally broken," Isshiki protested to me vehemently, tugging at my sleeve.

Gently escaping from her grasp, I made to defend my sister—more or less. "Well, rambling about a bunch of BS can be, like, a way she hides her shyness...," I said.

Yukinoshita nodded *mm-hmm* with deep interest, putting a hand to her chin. "She resembles you in that way, Hikigaya," she murmured with a wry smile.

"But it's not cute when Hikki does it...," Yuigahama said, kinda put off.

Isshiki snorted. "It's not cute when Okome-chan does it, either."

"Hmph! Oh, but if Komachi sulks here, then it makes it seem like I think I'm cute, and that's a low Komachi score..."

"Seriously, listen to this girl..."

With that above-it-all composure seniors are wont to have, we watched Komachi and Isshiki teasing each other again. *Mm-hmm, they're getting along. Very good.*

Then suddenly, Yukinoshita checked all our cups and rose to her feet without a word. Noticing that, Yuigahama rummaged around in her bag and brought out more snacks to empty onto the plate. And I, just like always, turned the page of the paperback I was reading.

"Oh, Komachi'll help with the tea, too," Komachi said.

"Oh? Well then, how about we do it together?" Yukinoshita replied.

While overhearing their conversation, I happened to look around, sweeping my gaze over the clubroom.

The rays of the inclining sun had grown much redder, coloring the steam for the tea, and for just a brief moment, it created a warm spot of sunlight in this clubroom.

Yuigahama was yoinking and munching snacks, Isshiki was facedown on her desk, exhausted and weary, Yukinoshita was instructing Komachi in detail on how to make the tea, and Komachi was a little weirded out by her manner of direction.

On the table were the familiar Western teacup and the mug with the dog printed on it. In my hands was the Japanese cup, and then there were the still brand-new matching mugs.

At some point, the cups had changed number and form, and even the sights in this room were changing.

I could imagine half a year ahead, but I didn't know about one year ahead. Two or three years in the future, or flying across greater intervals like ten years down the line, there probably wouldn't remain a single sign that we'd been here.

But—

Right after I'd thought that, a fragrant aroma wafted across the room.

When I looked for its source, I saw Komachi pouring tea under Yukinoshita's tutelage.

Yukinoshita folded her arms and narrowed her eyes, scrupulously observing every single move of Komachi's. Though Komachi was slightly in awe of that gaze, she was slowly pouring the tea with neat and careful gestures.

Eventually, this scene would be lost as well, and everything about this room would change.

But even so, I'm sure.

I'm sure the scent of tea in this room will stay the same.

Afterword

Good evening. This is Wataru Watari. Today, as always, I am sending you this afterword from the fifth floor of Shogakukan, Jinbo-cho, Kanda Hitotsubashi, in Tokyo.

This may be sudden, but have you all realized?

As of March 2021, it's been ten years since the publication of Volume 1 of *My Youth Romantic Comedy Is Wrong, As I Expected.*

It's the tenth anniversary! Ten years!

Since it's the long-awaited tenth anniversary, I considered writing at length in this afterword about my memories of these past ten years, random topics, or behind-the-scenes industry info while dropping insider dirt in a semi-accusatory way, or talking myself up to assert dominance, but if I did that, I'd never get done my whole life. When you talk about yourself, it will always go into a loop at some point. Uh-oh, if you keep me from blabbing about myself to show off and assert dominance, then I have nothing to write about at all… But for now, I'll write something.

Anyway, when you say ten years, it feels like a very long time, but when you're in the middle of desperately living it, it doesn't feel that way at all. I'd even say I'm the kind of cringey old guy who still thinks of himself as being in his twenties, though I am clearly and thoroughly aging, and I feel the cruelty of time. Heart palpitations and shortness of breath—it's bad.

It really does feel like ten years have passed without my even realizing it, but if I'd been saying at the start "I'll work hard for ten years *zoi*," I'm sure I never would have made it this far. When there's work in front of me that I have to do, I do it. Once you get that done, the next bit of work is lying there just a little ways away, so you trudge over to that and finish it again. Then there's some more a bit farther on again and you do it all over, and then before you know it, you've come a long way.

My schedule and list of tasks are basically always packed full, and when you've got work planned for the next two years or so, you come to spend all your energy on the now, and you don't have the mental space to think about the future. No time for tomorrow when yesterday was the deadline…

But even so, once you finish a job and reach a break, once you come to a turning point—for just a brief while, in the moment you take that break—sometimes your thoughts turn to the future.

"A year from now…well, work, I guess. In three years will probably also be work. In ten years… I dunno," I mutter with a wry smile as I once again set to the work in front of me.

It may be that he and she and she, and also he and she as well, are like that. If I can, though, I would like to get a glimpse of him and the girls in the future at some point. In one year, two years, ten years…I wonder how they'll be doing?

And so, on that note, this has been *My Youth Romantic Comedy Is Wrong, As I Expected*, Volume 14.5.

It's been a long time since I last wrote a short story collection, so how has this one, with its sequel-ish sort of stories, been?

There are other sort-of-sequel-like stories like this that I've written about in the anthology books *My Youth Romantic Comedy Is Wrong, As I Expected: Yukino Side*, *My Youth Romantic Comedy Is Wrong, As I Expected: On Parade*, *My Youth Romantic Comedy Is Wrong, As I Expected: Yui Side*, and *My Youth Romantic Comedy Is Wrong, As I Expected: All Stars*. Make sure to read them!

Also, there's the after story about which I've lied that it's a completely new legit sequel series post-finale: *My Youth Romantic Comedy*

Is Wrong, As I Expected: Shin, and this is a bonus for the TV anime *My Youth Romantic Comedy Is Wrong, As I Expected: Climax* Blu-ray and DVD release, so please do grab that!

And then and then, being published simultaneously with this volume 14.5 is the *My Youth Romantic Comedy Is Wrong, As I Expected: Ponkan⑧ ART WORKS,* what you'd commonly call an art book, of holy Ponkan⑧'s artwork! I would absolutely love it if you were to get this to look back on the ten-year history with. You know, if I might also add, a talk between holy Ponkan⑧ and myself is also in there! So please do!

Also, just between you and me, I'm working on a new project called *Oregairu Ketsu.* Nobody in the world knows the details about this yet, but I very much hope you will wait for more news. I want to talk about it soon; I want to talk ASAP about the things that often come up in that project.

So anyhow, I would be glad if you would stick with me a little while longer in this world as it expands a bit more.

And below, the acknowledgments:

Holy Ponkan⑧. My god! You're always so godly. Thank you for your work as usual, and for putting out the art book at the same time. It really makes me feel once more the weight and accumulation of ten long years. Thinking back on it, we've known each other for a long time, and I will be counting on you for a long time to come, too. Thank you very much.

My editor, Hoshino. Look! We had plenty of time this time, too! Ga-ha-ha! What can I say about it but "Ga-ha-ha, ga-ha-ha!" I dunno anything about plans for next time, but we're definitely totally fine for then, too! Ga-ha-ha! I'm obliged for your efforts, thank you very much. Ga-ha-ha!

To everyone involved with each part of the media franchise: You've helped me with so much different media, with the *Kan* anime first and foremost. This content continuing over ten long years is thanks to all your efforts. Truly, thank you very much. I will continue to count on you in the future.

And to all my readers. I am able to write stories about him and the girls again like this because of all your support. And it's not just for this—it's through all your support these past ten years that I've managed to make it this far, somehow. Honestly, thank you so much. I would be glad if I could receive your support in the future as well. *Oregairu* exists because of you!

And so on that note, I'll end it here for now. Next time, let's meet again in some kind of *Oregairu*!

On a certain day in March, facing the next ten years, while restoring my energy with MAX Coffee,

Wataru Watari

Chapter 1 ⋯ Always and forevermore, **Komachi Hikigaya** wants a sister-in-law.

P. 3   **"Every New Year is a milestone in your journey to the underworld."** Hachiman seems to be misremembering this poem by Sojun Ikkyuu, a Buddhist monk born in the fourteenth century. Instead of naming the New Year directly, the poem refers to the *kadomatsu* (New Year's pine decoration) used as a metaphor for New Year's. And the "milestone" used in the translation is actually an *ichirizuka*, mounds of earth separated by a distance of one *ri* (about 4 km). They often had pines planted on them.

P. 3   The name Ikkyuu could also be read as *hitoyasumi*, meaning "taking a break."

P. 3   **Godiego** is a rock band, and they have a song titled "Beautiful Name" (in English), which repeats the (English) refrain of "Every child has a beautiful name."

P. 3   **"*Kya-ha!* Lucky me! Time to have another normal year!"** Hachiman is adopting the manner of Raki Kiseki from *Aikatsu!*

P. 3 *"Don't rush, don't rush, a break here, a break there..."* is from the 1970s anime *Ikkyuu-san* about the life of the aforementioned monk Sojun Ikkyuu.

P. 4 **"This *purimiamu Japaniizu burando* product automatically celebrates the *Niuu Iyaa* on its own, no mess, no fuss!"** The original Japanese here is, more literally, "The *Japanese brand* flowing through this *body* celebrates the *New Year's ceremony* on its own," with the italicized words all being English. The particular words dropped—especially "this body"—is a reference to the language used by the TV shopping service Japanet Takata, which overseas audiences might be familiar with from the parody Jikanet Tanaka in the Persona series.

P. 4 **"After being swept along in the waves of shrinegoers (without being scolded from a distance)..."** This is a reference to the lyrics of "Graduation Photograph" by Yumi Arai: "You occasionally scold me from a distance / when I'm swept along by the crowds and change."

P. 6 **"'How dare you...' Komachi muttered scarily like a certain young environmentalist."** Greta Thunberg said this in 2019 at the UN's Climate Action Summit in New York.

P. 7 **"...like Solar Flare... *Tien Shinhan*..."** Solar Flare is a move of Tien Shinhan in *Dragon Ball*.

Chapter 2 ··· Nevertheless, **Komachi Hikigaya** won't give up on getting a sister-in-law.

P. 12 **"You could call that mission complete. You could get a reward to use on a gacha pull."** *Complete* in a gacha game (using the English term) refers to getting all the items of a random set, after which they give you some of the in-game currency that costs real money. Some kind of rock is typical, which is why Hachiman cites a stone as the reward in the original.

P. 12 **"I was just about to attend to some lucky bag gacha…"** Lucky bags are common New Year's items sold in Japan in all different kinds of stores, from clothing shops to cafés. They have a random assortment of items of varying value.

P. 13 **"Learn from the prime minister's cherry-blossom-event invitation list."** The governmental "cherry blossom viewing party" was an annual event that had been expanded every year to invite a variety of politicians and influential people, all on the taxpayers' dime. In 2019, it came under fire for lack of transparency about who was invited and was canceled.

P. 13 **"Hey? Could you stop talking about my marriage like this is a duel? Even if you send your big bro to the graveyard, you can't summon a big sister."** Hachiman is referencing the *Yu-Gi-Oh!* card game here.

P. 16 **Treasured Tool** is a term for special weapons in the Fate universe.

Chapter 3 ⋯ And then the **festival** ends, and a new **festival** begins.

P. 19 **"…or get on a portable shrine and call out *wasshoi, wasshoi* like Mirai Moriyama in *Moteki*…"** This is a reference to the opening of the drama *Moteki* in which the protagonist, played by Mirai Moriyama, is raised up on a *mikoshi* (a portable shrine used in festivals) by a bunch of girls.

P. 19 **"Chiba is famous for festivals and dancing. There are idiots who dance and idiots who watch, so if you're an idiot like the rest, you've got to dance and sing a song."** Calling back to the cultural festival in Vol. 6, this is a variation on "Chiba Ondo," punning on the ending with *odoranakya sing-a-song* instead of *odoranakya son son!* (you miss out if you don't dance).

P. 22 *"I'll power-snooze my way through it just like Meng Haoran!"*
Meng Haoran was a Tang dynasty poet. Hachiman is probably referring to the poem "Chūn Xiǎo," meaning "Spring Dawn," which, trans-
lated roughly, goes, "I enjoy sleeping comfortably through the spring
dawn / I can hear twittering of birds here and there / It reminds me I
heard awful wind and rain last night / I wonder how much the flower
petals have fallen?"

P. 23 **"Rarely but often happens"** is the familiar meme from the famous
FFXI player Buronto.

P. 24 **"Ah-ha, so she's the type of *umamusume* who's good taking the
lead from behind? She totally blew right past me at the end."** *Umamusume: Pretty Derby* is a cell phone game about racehorses reincar-
nated as pretty girls in another world. There's also an anime.

P. 29 **"...and Yukino Bijin from Tracen Academy."** Yukino Bijin is one of
the girls from *Umamusume*.

P. 32 **" ...*GoYuu* are basically already together..."** Satoru Gojo and Yuji
Itadori are a popular ship in the anime *Jujutsu Kaisen*.

P. 36 **"Like the Glay two-hundred-thousand-person concert."** Hachiman
is referring to Glay Expo '99 Survival. Glay is a rock band that's been
active since 1988, too.

P. 37 **BanNam Fest** (Bandai Namco Entertainment Festival), **Anisama**
(Animelo Summer Live) and **Lantis Matsuri** are all *otaku*-related
music events.

P. 38 **"...they call the first song 'Daihatsu.'"** This is a thing with
Aikatsu! concerts—they play a song called "Diamond Happy" first

because it can be abbreviated to "Daihatsu," which could also mean "first thing."

P. 38 "...just *emotional.* Ah, soooo eeeee...eeeemo..." This is based on an Internet meme, what you'd originally expect from the drawn out *eeeee* is *ero* (sexy).

P. 38 "...eating the emo-emo fruit..." This references the devil fruit from *One Piece*, which grant people special powers upon eating them. They're usually called things like *gomu-gomu* fruit or *mera-mera* fruit.

P. 41 "But it's only me, Bump of Chicken, and people on drugs who try to see things that cannot be seen." "Trying to see things that can't be seen" is a line from Bump of Chicken's song "Tentai Kansoku" (Observing heavenly bodies).

P. 41 "...makes you feel like the protagonist of a Makoto Shinkai film. You get theme music in your head and everything." In the original, he specifically mentions Masayoshi Yamazaki, who did the theme song "One More Time, One More Chance" for Makoto Shinkai's film *5 Centimeters per Second*.

P. 42 "Like *Vaaanilla Vanilla Vaaanilla whoo whoo* sorta thing?" Vanilla is the name of a recruiting service for sex work businesses. They park their trucks in downtown areas and have barkers that call out "Vaaanillaaaaa!" In some regions, the Vanilla truck doesn't appear, depending on local noise / public nuisance bylaws.

P. 42 "...it's that thing where you go "Umapyoi! Umapyoi!" in a winning live..." A winning live is the scene at the end of an *Umamusume* playthrough once you're done raising your horse girl, and they do an idol-style dance with a pop song. *Umapyoi* is a word made up by

Umamusume that means a variety of things, but it's also in the lyrics of some of the songs and is used as a fan chant.

P. 43   **"One, two! Yeeeah, yeeeah, yeah yeah yeah!"** This chant—*Hai, seeno! Haaai haaai hai hai hai!*—is used mostly for idol groups such as Nogizaka46, Sakurazaka46, and Hinatazaka46. They're similar to AKB48.

P. 47   **"Whoaaa! Queeeen!"** Here, Tobe actually says "Toutomi Hideyoshi," which is a play on the word *toutoi*. Literally meaning "precious," *toutoi* is generally used in a similar manner to the more dated *moe*—just a word you say about your favorite character or idol in an *otaku* context. Toyotomi Hideyoshi is a famous general from the Sengoku era, and using his name is just a form of net slang that was popular around the time this book was written.

P. 49   **No reply. It's just a corpse** is a standard dialogue line when investigating dead bodies in the Dragon Quest series.

P. 51   *Spelunker* is a 1983 platformer, originally on the Atari. Like many games of the era, there was a lot of dying.

P. 51   **"...a radio that's breaking down and you can't hear anything from is somewhat preferable... Wait, if you can't hear anything from it, that's not breaking down. Isn't that just broken?"** This is a reference to the lyrics of the 1990 pop song by Hideaki Tokunaga, "Kowarekake no Radio." He's misremembering them, though, since in the song, it isn't the radio you can't hear anything from, but himself: "My body won't hear anything, won't listen to anything... Teach me true happiness, radio that's breaking down."

P. 54   **"Oh-hooo, verily sooo?"** *Ee, hontou ni gozaru kaa?* is a quote from Sasaki Kojirou / Assassin in the Fate franchise.

Chapter 4 ⋯ Nonchalantly, casually, **Iroha Isshiki** assembles a future.

P. 65 **"I Want to Make Miracles with You"** is the title of a pop song by the band Sambomaster.

P. 66 **"So you're Machi Tawara, huh?"** Waaaay back in Volume 2, Hachiman brought up this tanka by the poet Machi Tawara: "So you said to me, / 'I like this flavor a lot,' / so, well, that means the / sixth of July is now the / salad anniversary." This line is also worded like the *Pop Team Epic* meme "So you're an anti, huh?"

P. 68 **The Straw Millionaire** is an old folktale, probably written in the Heian period, about a poor man who starts with a piece of straw and trades up over and over until he becomes wealthy.

Chapter 5 ⋯ But surely, **the girls** will also continue to go wrong.

P. 75 **"...on the metaphorical conveyor belt of conversation..."** The original line here was "finding the right moments to place [words from] the *sa* column like a work operation." All his stock replies in Japanese start with *sa*, and he's also punning "*sa* column" (*sagyou*) with "work operation" (*sagyou*). As you can imagine, this is wildly untranslatable.

P. 80 *"The most popular is, of course, this one, Komachi Hikigaya* and *She's the classmate I'm most looking forward to seeing more of! I hope she gives it all she's got!* and then she'd be the favorite to win the race." This is probably a reference to the idol game *Umamusume.*

P. 83 **"Since both our parents have the inheritance factors 'Corporate slave ☆☆☆,' at this rate, I'll wind up inheriting that, too."** More *Umamusume.* This is part of the inheritance system, where a girl can become a "parent" to a trainee who will inherit her traits.

P. 91   *"Wow, that Okome-chan nickname has actually stuck... Maybe I'll call her Rice-chan at home, too! But Rice-chan won't call me 'Brother' in that refined and respectful way."* Isshiki calls Komachi "Okome-chan" because of the brand of rice (*okome*) called Akita Komachi. But here Hachiman is talking about a character from *Umamusume*, Rice Shower, who calls the player *onii-sama*, a respectful term for "big brother."

P. 92   **"Komachi is simply conducting herself as the club president. Komachi wouldn't designate this as an impression of Yukino."** **"Ohhh, you nailed it—she does talk pretentiously like that."** In Japanese, Komachi ends both sentences with *nodakeredo*, which is Yukino's verbal tic in Japanese, but it has no direct meaning in English; it does communicate a certain haughty formality.

P. 93   **"...Komachi briskly poured the black tea into the cups—she was hardly green at this, after all (ha-ha)."** The original line here is "'briskly poured it (since it's tea),' punning "brisk" (*chaccha*) and "tea" (*ocha*).

P. 93   *"Mm, I'm feeling great today, and the tea is, too..."* "I'm feeling great today, and this cigarette tastes good" is an old ad slogan from Ikoi brand cigarettes, which sold tobacco products in Japan from the 1950s to 1970s. Hachiman is being a little witty here, because the word commonly used to take a puff of a cigarette (*ippuku*) is also less commonly used for taking a sip of tea.

P. 95   **"She was shrugging like Tora-san going,** *If you're gonna tell me that, it's over.***"** Tora-san is the protagonist of the long-running film series Otoko wa Tsurai yo (It's tough being a man) from the 1960s, last referenced in Vol. 9. "If you're gonna tell me that, it's over" is the line he says in every film once his uncle finally snaps at him, and he leaves on a journey.

P. 100 **"Oh my, all aboard the SS KomaIro."** In Japanese, Hachiman is literally saying "Oh my, how nice," but in a very feminine manner, referencing a meme for what *yuri* fans say when they see *yuri* content.

P. 104 **"After seeing his footwork, [the shoryuuken] was easy"** is a quote from the fighting game legend Daigo Umehara.

P. 105 **"...yesterday that our drum-type washing machine has a mysterious 'air iron' function. Oh look, another function I won't touch with a ten-foot pole."** The original Japanese for this last line is punning on *kinou* (function) and *kinou* (yesterday).

P. 107 **"Third year of middle school—in other words, fifteen years old—is the age when you race out on a stolen bike and go around breaking the windows of the school at night."** The first half of this is referencing the previously mentioned lyrics of the song "Juugo no Yoru" (A Night at 15) by the late Yutaka Ozaki, which describes racing out on a stolen bike at night when he's fifteen, as well as other delinquent behavior. He does not talk about breaking windows, however.

P. 107 **"But what does it all meeeeean?"** This line from *Naruto* was originally just Naruto saying, "What do you mean?" but then it turned into a meme on Futaba Channel. There were a number of nonsensical memes only understood by insiders ("It's Izanami"; "It's become a sacrifice"), prompting people who weren't in on the joke to respond with this line, which then became a meme in its own right.

P. 110 **"...got herself pumped up. Zoi!"** This references *ganbaru zoi*, the cutesy but meaningless sentence-ending *zoi* from the protagonist of the manga *New Game!* when she tries to get herself motivated for her day.

P. 111 **"Komachi and Isshiki both went 'Mumu!' like the Rakuten Card Man, attention fully on me."** This is from an ad campaign for the online shopping site Rakuten. The Rakuten Card Man has cards for eyes, staring straight at the viewer as he goes "Mumu!"

P. 117 **"This is the birth of the Full-Wallet Alchemist."** The original Japanese here was *kogane no renkinjutsushi*, meaning "pocket change alchemist," in reference to the manga by Hiromu Arakawa, *Hagane no Renkinjutsushi* (*Fullmetal Alchemist*).